# The Sound of Summer Voices

# The Sound of Summer Voices

## HELEN TUCKER

STEIN AND DAY/*Publishers*/New York

*For my mother*
Helen Welch Tucker
*and to the memory of my father*
William Blair Tucker

# 1

It was at the beginning of the summer of his eleventh
year that Patrick Quincannon Tolson reluctantly
came to the conclusion that one of his aunts—either
Athena or Beryl—was not his aunt at all but his
mother. This new knowledge (for as soon as an
idea stayed in his mind for a while it crossed the line
from speculation to knowledge) pained him deeply,
for it meant that throughout his whole, entire life
everybody had formed a conspiracy against him and
had lied to him. Not only Athena and Beryl, but
even Uncle Darius, who was always saying that the
worst thing in the whole, entire world was a liar.
("Listen, boy, if you tell stories, one of these days
when you approach the Heavenly Gates that great
archangel up there is going to point a finger at
you and say, 'No liar shall enter therein.' You remember that while you're living, and it will make
things a lot easier for you when you're dead.")

No sooner had the pain of being duped by his
three living relatives subsided somewhat than he was
struck by a new and greater pain. He had been
dumb-stupid enough to have been taken in by their
lies for eleven years. To see himself in this light—
no smarter than a cretin—was the biggest hurt of
all.

They probably would have gone on lying to him
and getting away with it for the rest of his natural

life if it had not been for Rusty Nichols. Rusty set him straight about a lot of things. During recess on next to the last day of school, Rusty had told him where babies came from. Not only where, but how. Patrick listened attentively before he began scoffing. After all, Rusty was only *nine* years old so what did he know?

When Rusty had finished his revelation, Patrick pulled himself up straight, brushed his brown hair away from his forehead, and in his best imitation of Uncle Darius, said, "That's a lot of cock and bull. Rusty Nichols, you're making that up out of your head."

But even as he scoffed, he mulled over Rusty's words. It might just be that Rusty had some information that he himself did not have. What Rusty had said was crazy-fantastic enough to be true. Sometimes, he knew, the craziest things turned out to be the truest.

His enlightenment caused him to look at everyone he knew in a different way, and after this scrutiny no one turned out to be the same person Patrick had seen and known before. Not even Mavis, who had been cooking for the Quincannon family for years and years and who never under any circumstances had been known to change at all.

Thinking about Mavis reminded Patrick that she, also, was in on the conspiracy. She had played along with the stories that Athena, Beryl, and Uncle Darius had told him about his mother, and since Mavis had been working for them so long, she certainly knew they were stories.

On the day school was out he spent the afternoon on the steps of the back porch trying to get everything straight in his mind before he began to make accusations. At one point he heard Athena in the kitchen asking Mavis, "Have you seen Patrick?"

"He's sitting out yonder," Mavis said.

"What's he doing?"

"Just sitting. I guess he's lonesome thinking about no school for a long time."

Athena gave her half-laugh (if she had a whole-laugh, Patrick had never heard it). "You know better than that, Mavis. All of the little devils inside him are holding a summit conference now to plan the summer strategy. When Patrick is sitting quietly, beware of what's to come."

Later, just before dark, he came to the only possible answer. Like a careful geneticist, he had traced in his mind his own beginning, and what he came up with was exactly opposed to what he had been told.

He knew the Quincannon history well. In fact, everyone in Laurelton knew it, because the Quincannons has been there as long as the town had. He often wondered why he was always referred to as "one of the Quincannons" when his last name was Tolson, but he supposed it was because he was related to the family. However, it did give him pause to be called "the last of the Quincannons." It was like being called the last of the Mohicans, and one thing he did know for sure was that he wasn't a cotton-picking Indian, although at the moment the idea appealed to him.

His concern right now was not with his early ancestors, but with the last two generations. Uncle

Darius Quincannon (who was Patrick's great-uncle) and his twin brother, Donald, had been born in the rambling old house where Patrick lived now. Darius never married, but Donald married a Laurelton girl and they had three daughters (or so Patrick had been told), Athena, Beryl, and Celinda. Donald and Sarah were killed one Sunday afternoon while out for a drive, and Darius became the guardian of the Quincannon money, house, and three little girls.

This was what Patrick had been told from the time he was a baby, and so the story had an air of mystery and mythology about it. Celinda Quincannon, the youngest of the three girls (so the story went) was his mother. She was, Patrick gathered from things he had heard Athena say, a bit on the wild side, and she eloped with a man Uncle Darius did not like when she was eighteen years old. She stayed away for almost a year and then came home two months before Patrick was born. Three days after his birth, she died.

That was what they said, and since he had known nothing else but to believe what he was told, he believed. Now he knew better.

There never was and never had been a Celinda Quincannon. She had been made up by Uncle Darius and Athena and Beryl for Patrick's benefit. After all, if there had been a Celinda, there would be somewhere in the house or the town some evidence of her existence, but there was none. There was not a picture, a memento, not *any*thing that anyone had ever pointed to and said, "This belonged to your mother." In the family album there were pictures of his grandfather Donald and his grandmother Sarah with their two little girls, Athena and Beryl, but there was no Celinda. There were pictures of Uncle Darius—one of him with Beryl in her white graduation dress, and one with Athena sitting beside him in the swing on the front porch. But there was no picture of Celinda because Celinda never existed. No one in school or Sunday school, in the whole, entire town, had ever mentioned Celinda's name to him. Now that he thought about it, that in itself spoke volumes, because one thing people in Laurelton liked to do better than anything else was to talk.

The way he had it figured—now that he knew all about babies and everything—was that either Athena or Beryl had done something wrong, that a girl is never supposed to do until she is old and married, and he, Patrick, was the result. Of course, Uncle Darius would never tell him that he had come into this world as the aftermath of sin and scandal (sin committed by a *Quincannon* woman, at that), and so the story of Celinda had been dreamed up by the three of them, Uncle Darius and his two aunts.

And now he had to find out which of his aunts was really his mother. They were both old. Athena was thirty-five and Beryl was thirty-two, and neither had married because (he had figured this out, too) the shame of one of them had shamed them both so they couldn't go out and get husbands the way other girls did. Probably everybody in Laurelton *knew* and nobody would marry them.

All of this sort of made hash out of Uncle Darius' high-toned words about liars and lying, didn't it? He had let Patrick grow up believing a lie, and Athena and Beryl had helped him.

And to think that even Mavis had deceived him! He had always thought Mavis was his friend, and he had always told her everything, and when she talked to him he knew he was hearing the gospel truth because Mavis was very religious and went to church every Sunday. Sometimes she even preached in church. He knew this for a fact, because she had taken him with her once when she was "holding down the pulpit," and he had sat on the front row looking up at this different Mavis, her brown face clashing somewhat with the black robe she wore, while she charged the brethren to "believe on Jesus and live the good life."

He shifted on the hard stone step and looked back toward the kitchen where Mavis had lifted her voice in song. "I'm going to tell that wondrous story, when I wake, wake, wake up in Glory."

He folded his arms across his knees and rested his head on his arms. It was getting dark now, and he was tired as all get-out. This thinking, this *finding out*, had exhausted him, but he still had to come up with a way to make all of them admit the truth. He could not just walk in the house and demand that they tell him the truth, because he knew exactly what they'd say. "Why, Patrick, whatever are you talking about? You do come up with the queerest notions sometimes." He would have to play it smart and either trap them into telling him or find out for himself.

He heard Athena call him from an upstairs window, but he did not answer immediately.

"Patrick, I know you're down there. Come on in now and get washed up for supper."

Slowly, he got up and went across the porch and

into the kitchen where Mavis was putting a pan of biscuits in the oven. She straightened up and was about to speak to him when suddenly he raised his right arm and pointed at her.

"No liar shall enter therein," he thundered.

Mavis closed her mouth and stared at him for a minute, then she shook her head. "Lord, Patrick, Miss Athena was right. And this is only the beginning of summer."

In his room at the top of the stairs, Patrick left the door open while he changed his shirt. One of Athena's steadfast rules was a clean shirt every night, or no supper. He moved about the room quietly, trying to hear the voices downstairs. It was important now that he hear the things they said when he was not in their presence.

The front door slammed, and he knew that Uncle Darius and Beryl had come in. Every afternoon Uncle Darius went to the dress shop where Beryl worked and walked home with her. The Lord knew that Beryl was certainly old enough to find her way home, a distance of two and a half blocks, by herself, but apparently the Lord had not yet given this knowledge to Uncle Darius, who always said that ladies did not walk the streets unescorted after five o'clock. This invariably brought the same comment from

Beryl: "Ladies don't go out and work all day either, Uncle Darius. At least, not the kind of ladies you're talking about." Uncle Darius' only answer to that was a loud "Hummph! (Mumble, mumble) Remember, my girl, blood will always tell."

Now that he gave the matter some thought, Patrick realized that Uncle Darius had very definite opinions on almost everything. He had never heard the old man say, "I don't know," or "Let me think about that for a while," when asked a question. Uncle Darius answered questions the way some preachers read scripture, as though there could be no doubt that he was backed by no lesser authority than God.

Patrick had seen him stand in the center of the living room time after time, his thin white hair in disarray, his gaunt cheeks sucked in, as he delivered his opinions to his two nieces and his great-nephew.

There were a lot of things in the world which Uncle Darius "refused to tolerate." This was, Patrick knew, his way of saying he hated all liars, Yankees, casseroles and pastry, Catholics, women who giggled, and Laurelton businessmen who wanted to bring Yankee industry into town. He didn't exactly cotton to Jews either, but since there was only one Jewish family in Laurelton, he didn't worry much about them.

Right now Uncle Darius was on a real Yankee hate-kick because some Yankees who had moved a textile plant to Laurelton were trying to buy the Quincannon property and have it rezoned from residential to business.

"Not while there's breath left in my body," Uncle Darius stormed. "The Quincannons have always lived here and they always will." He looked apprehensively at Athena and Beryl. "I don't know what you girls will do with this place after I'm gone. The younger generation has no respect for tradition any more—no respect for anything. But if you sell to those scoundrels, I'll. . . ." He did not finish the threat, but added, "You can't trust anyone who lives north of Richmond, Virginia."

Darius Quincannon's stubbornness was a sore spot in Laurelton. Patrick had heard his aunts talking about it, and he got the idea that they wouldn't mind selling the house and grounds and moving into a smaller, more modern house in a better section of town. Although the section where they lived had been the best at the time the house was built, the business district had grown so much that it now entirely surrounded the Quincannon property, which consisted of three acres of trees, vines, and underbrush right in the heart of town. An iron fence covered with thick ivy was all that separated the inhabitants of the house from busy Main Street.

The house itself was close to the front of the property. It was a three-storied, nondescript-colored frame building always in need of paint. "The perfect retreat," Beryl had said once, "for impoverished gentility."

At one time the land behind the house had been a huge flower garden where the early Quincannons had grown azaleas, roses, camellias, iris, and jonquils. Now it was a miniature jungle of oaks, elms, magnolias, and poison ivy. Just looking at the thick growth from the back porch was enough to frighten Patrick, although he had, once or twice, wandered through the little wood to prove to himself that he wasn't a scaredy-cat.

But Patrick was more in sympathy with Uncle Darius than with Athena and Beryl. You ought not to let Yankees run you away from your home. He had said as much to Uncle Darius.

"You have spoken a parable, boy. Not while there's breath in my body. . . ." He hesitated and gave Patrick a strange look. "And not while the earthly remains of one Quincannon lie buried in this land."

Face and hands washed, clean shirt on, Patrick tiptoed down the stairs and sat on the bottom step facing the massive front door with its tiny stained-glass side windows. On his right was the dining room where Mavis was putting supper on the table, and on his left was the living room where Uncle Darius was expounding, disappointingly, on nothing more important than the weather.

"They are predicting that this will be the hottest summer since the weather bureau started keeping records, and it may be at that if today is any indication."

"Thank heavens the shop is air-conditioned," Beryl said. "Although it makes the house seem hotter when I get home."

"It isn't too bad," Athena said. "I imagine I'll be too busy keeping up with Patrick to notice the weather. That boy—I just don't know."

"What's the matter with him?" Uncle Darius asked.

Patrick leaned forward.

Athena sighed. "Nothing. But I'm always better

satisfied when he's in school. There's not enough around here to keep him occupied during the summer."

"We could send him to camp somewhere," Beryl said. "I think he might enjoy that."

"No," Uncle Darius said. "Patrick is going to stay right here. He can help me with my paste-ups."

Patrick gritted his teeth. That was a devil of a way to spend the summer. Every morning Uncle Darius took yesterday's newspaper and cut out stories he thought showed history-in-the-making and pasted them in a large scrapbook. "The newspapers are the only means of recording the events that will later be historical," he had said, "and future generations will thank me for giving them the opportunity to read about these events when they were written up in their proper perspective." At last count, there were forty-seven scrapbooks of clippings in a corner in the attic. Uncle Darius had been at it for years— even before he retired from the bank.

"I think Mavis has supper on," Athena said. "I'd better see what's keeping Patrick."

Patrick stood up quickly and went to the dining room. Perhaps while they were eating he could think of a way to find out the things he had to know.

"Oh, Patrick, here you are," Athena said when they entered the dining room. "I thought you were still upstairs."

Patrick stood silently beside her chair at the foot of the long table while Uncle Darius seated Beryl at the right before taking his place at the head of the table. Patrick sat across from Beryl.

After asking the blessing, Uncle Darius looked

up brightly at Patrick and said, "Well, I suppose you're ebullient tonight, my boy, at the prospect of vacation stretching before you, but I must say you don't look it. Why are you scowling so? Well, never mind, tomorrow I'll see if I can't find enough for you to do so you won't have time to scowl. I have a little job. . . ."

Patrick stopped listening and concentrated on the wheat pattern on the plate in front of him. When he glanced across the table, he thought he saw Beryl wink at him but he wasn't sure.

Athena was serving the plates. "You will have a lamb chop, won't you, Patrick?"

Why did she always ask if he would have something when she knew good and well she was going to make him eat it whether he wanted it or not? He loathed lamb.

"Yes, thank you."

Athena always sat bolt upright in her chair, as though she were sitting on one of those Hindu nail boards. She was tall and angular with wiry auburn hair and bright blue eyes that seemed to snap when she blinked. There was not the slightest resemblance between her and Beryl. Beryl was softer looking. She had blonde hair and faded blue eyes like an old china doll Patrick had seen in the attic which Beryl had said belonged to her when she was a little girl.

He had never dared ask himself which of his aunts he liked better, because he had been made to understand early in life that a little gentleman, even if he had a preference, was never supposed to show it. The truth was, he was a little in awe of both of them, but somehow Beryl seemed nearer his age, more of a pal, while Athena had always been five years older than God—closer to Uncle Darius' age.

Suddenly he looked at Uncle Darius and without preliminaries asked, "What did my mother look like and why don't we have any pictures of her?"

Uncle Darius, his fork almost to his mouth, laid the fork down on his plate. "Patrick, we've described your mother to you any number of times. You know that." He did not answer nor make reference to the second part of the question.

Doggedly Patrick continued, "Did she look like you, Athena?"

"Cee looked more like me, dear," Beryl said. "But she was much prettier. She had the most beautiful brown eyes I've ever seen, and her hair was so pale that it was almost silver."

"Then why've I got brown hair?"

There was a silence, then Athena said, "How did it go today, Beryl? I don't suppose the summer slump has set in yet."

See, Patrick told himself almost gleefully, I was right all the time. They wouldn't even discuss it with him. Before Beryl could answer, he said, "Did my father have brown hair?"

"He had dark hair," Beryl said. "I don't remember the exact shade."

"Do I look like him?"

"Patrick," Uncle Darius pushed himself up a bit on the arms of his chair, "why are you asking all these unnecessary questions? We have told you about your mother, and as for your father, the less said about him, the better. Now be quiet and eat your supper and let the adults get in a word now and then. Children should be seen . . ."

"And not heard," Patrick finished for him. "I just wondered, that's all. Did Jason Tolson live here in Laurelton?" They had told him his father's name many years ago, and that was all he knew about the man except that Uncle Darius did not like him and had had a fit when Celinda ran away with him. But now that he was convinced there had never been a Celinda, he wondered more and more about Jason Tolson.

"Jaybird Tolson never lived anywhere very long," Athena said. "Now eat, Patrick, or we'll send you upstairs."

Uncle Darius carved away on his lamb chop and at the same time uttered a slight humming noise. He often did this when he was deep in thought. Finally the humming stopped, and he said to no one in particular, "I'm not sure the boy is entirely well. Seems a bit off his feed to me. A bit pale."

"Nonsense, Uncle Darius." The half-laugh from Athena. "You know he's always milk-white, even when he's been in the sun. He may be a bit anemic. . . ."

Sometimes they discussed him like this, with him right there, as though he were a big blob of nothing, that couldn't see, hear, or think. Obediently, as though acting on an unspoken command, he closed his mind to their conversation and began to make plans for tomorrow. Tomorrow he would go to see Rusty Nichols and tell him his big secret, and maybe Rusty, who had turned out to be not so dumb-stupid after all, could help him find out which of his aunts was really his mother.

He looked down the table at Athena and then

across at Beryl. The Lord knew he could not imagine either one of them doing that thing Rusty had told him about, but one of them must have, or else they adopted him from an orphanage. He gave this thought considerable play in his mind and then discarded it. No, he could never have gotten into the Quincannon home and family that way. Two unmarried ladies and an old bachelor did not go around adopting orphans. Back to the original question: was it Athena or Beryl?

"If you have finished, Patrick, you may be excused," Uncle Darius said. "There are some things I want to talk over with the girls."

"I'll go talk to Mavis," he said, excusing himself and going from the dining room to the pantry. He stood just outside the swinging door; that way he could hear the things Uncle Darius was going to discuss.

"Well, they upped the ante today," Uncle Darius said. "They'll give us eighty thousand dollars for the privilege of doing us the favor of turning us out of our home."

Beryl whistled softly. "That's a lot of money."

"But not half enough for this property," Athena said. "It's a ridiculous offer."

"Any offer from them would be ridiculous," Uncle Darius said. "Ridiculous and unacceptable. We won't sell at any price."

Patrick left the pantry and went to the kitchen. They weren't going to talk about him after all, only about those Yankees who wanted to buy their land. The last thing he heard was Uncle Darius saying, "You wouldn't believe it, but there are people, Laurelton people, who think we should sell. Louis Nichols stopped me on the street today and insinuated he thought we were impeding the progress of the town by not selling. Said those people want to put an office building right here where the house is. Hummph!"

Mavis was sitting on a high, three-legged stool beside the kitchen cabinet, waiting to be called to clear the table. "You calmed down some now, Patrick?"

"I want to talk to you, Mavis," he said matter-of-factly.

"Speak quick then, because I want to get at those dishes and get away from here. I got a meeting tonight."

"Can I go to Meeting with you?" he asked. Suddenly the thought of going to Meeting with Mavis, standing beside her in the crowded church and singing "Love Lifted Me," appealed to him. It would be something sure in a world that had, in the past two days, become completely insane.

"No, you can't go," she said, fanning her ample lap with her apron. "I don't reckon you'd better go to church with me any more."

"Why not?"

"You're getting too big to go along with a nurse. Besides, you've got your own church to go to."

Patrick changed the subject abruptly. "Tell me about my father. Did you ever see Jason Tolson with your own eyes?"

Mavis hesitated. "Yes, I saw Jaybird a few times."

"Why do you all call him Jaybird?"

"Because that's what he was—a jaybird. Why

you suddenly want to know about him, Patrick? You know Mr. Darius don't want his name spoken in this house."

"Where is my father now?"

"That's enough about that, Patrick. I'm not going to let your curiosity get me in any trouble around here."

Patrick was thoughtful for a minute, then he decided to give her one more chance to come over to his side before he relegated her irrevocably to the battalions of the Enemy.

"Tell me about my mother then."

"I've told you about your mother, Patrick. All of us have. She was three years younger than Miss Beryl, and she was like her in a lot of ways, but she was different, too."

"Different how?"

"I don't know how. Just different. All three of the girls had different ways, but Miss Cee was the most different."

"Why doesn't anybody have a picture of her? I want to see what she looked like."

Mavis started to speak then apparently changed her mind. "She was just about the prettiest thing that ever lived," she said finally. "She looked like an angel with all that light hair shining around her head like a halo."

"If she was so pretty, why didn't anybody ever take her picture?" He was not going to let her get away with avoiding the question any longer.

"Go along now," Mavis said. "I think they're about through in there, and I can get to the dishes. I don't want to be late for my meeting."

He hadn't planned to show his hand so soon, but Mavis' lack of cooperation had made him mad. "You know what, Mavis? There never was any such person as Celinda Quincannon. You all just made her up. She never really lived and I'm not her son. So there. You can all stop lying to me now, because I *know*."

"Jesus God!" Mavis raised her hands, pink palms outstretched as though imploring heaven for help. "Patrick, you are plumb out of your mind."

"I know who my real mother is," he said. Maybe if he could make her think he knew, he could fool her into telling him something.

"Miss Athena's always said you got the wildest imagination in captivity, and I guess she's just about as right as she can be." Mavis got down from the stool, went to the sink and turned on the water full force, squirted soap from a plastic bottle, then concentrated on the rising bubbles. "You're just like your mother that way," she added in an almost inaudible tone.

The swinging door from the pantry shot outward and Athena towered above them in the room. "You can clear away now, Mavis. Patrick, have you done . . . oh, that's right, no more homework for a while. Well, maybe Beryl will play a game of gin rummy with you before you go to bed."

"I don't want to play," Patrick said. "I think I'll go to bed now. I'm tired."

Athena shrugged. "Suit yourself." Then to Mavis, "Maybe Uncle Darius is right. The boy could be sick."

Mavis shook her head. "No ma'am. I don't think so. Just growing pains, I guess."

"I don't have *any* pains," Patrick said. He turned his back on them abruptly and left the room.

As he was going up the stairs he heard Athena join Uncle Darius and Beryl in the living room, so he waited to hear what report she would give them about him.

"Mavis is going to another meeting at church tonight," she said. "This is the second one this week."

"That's better than having her go to a Black Muslim meeting or something like that," Beryl said.

"Have they started having those around here?" Athena asked.

"If they haven't, they will," Uncle Darius said. "It's those damn carpetbaggers from Up Yonder making all the trouble. They did it once and they're doing it again. Things are always all right until the Yankees move in. That's what I told Louis Nichols today when he kept on about why didn't we sell the house to those factory folks. I don't understand how those troublemakers could have fooled the people—people who've always lived in Laurelton—so completely. 'But we need their money, their business,' Louis said. I'll tell you what I think. . . ."

Patrick moved on up the stairs. He already knew what Uncle Darius thought on almost any given subject. And it was fairly certain that having gotten off on his favorite hate-kick, he would make no mention of Patrick or his questionable parentage.

He went to his room and closed the door. It was just possible that when he was young—too young to understand or care what they were talking about—they had talked and talked until they had exhausted the subject, and now they were all talked out and there was nothing new to say. This would mean that all the eavesdropping in the world wouldn't help him. He was going to have to find out for himself.

He undressed in the dark and put on his pajamas. He wasn't sure why he didn't want the light on, but for some reason the darkness, for once, did not scare him. It seemed almost friendly.

He went to the window that looked out over the back of the property and knelt on the window seat, pressing his forehead against the cool wire screen. Outside a cricket chirped and the woods lit up briefly here and there with the small yellow glistening of lightning bugs. Tomorrow he would paint a jar blue, and tomorrow night he would catch lightning bugs in it. Their lights looked so pretty shining through the blue glass. Maybe Rusty would help him. He did not want to go out there alone, especially at night.

He pressed his forehead deeper into the screen. There had been something in the back of his head all day that had been bothering him, and now he knew what it was. Remembering Uncle Darius' fight with the Yankee made him think of it. "Not while the earthly remains of one Quincannon lie buried in this land."

Deep in the woods, almost to where the iron fence joined Oak Street, was a white tombstone bearing the inscription, "Celinda, Beloved Daughter of Donald and Sarah Quincannon. *Requiescat in Pace.*"

He shivered as he thought about it. Celinda had been real after all because she was buried out there. But still, there was something funny-peculiar about that tombstone. He tried to remember what it was. He thought about the first time he had seen it, when he was just a little boy, and had asked Beryl about it, and she had said, "That's your mother's." (It had been the only thing that had ever been pointed out to him as belonging to his mother.) It hadn't occurred to him then that there was something different about the marker, because he had been only a kid. But now he compared it in his mind with other markers he had seen in the Laurelton cemetery, and he knew what the difference was. There were no dates—not a single date of any kind—on Celinda's tombstone.

Why? Every marker he had ever seen told when somebody was born and when he died. Why not Celinda's?

He left the window and rubbed his forehead where the screen had made small criss-crosses. Something was all wrong somewhere, and since there was no other explanation, his first idea certainly must be the right one. There was no date of birth because Celinda had never been born, and therefore she couldn't very well have died either. That tombstone out there was all part of the big lie everybody told him to keep him from finding out that Athena or Beryl was his real mother.

# 3

It was Saturday morning, but now that school was out, Saturday had lost its significance as a day of freedom and had become merely the day before Sunday.

Because the window in Patrick's room faced the east, the first glimmer of sunrise lit up the room like a rosy, spreading fire, which in summer burned brightly enough to awaken him at an early hour.

He sat up in bed and performed his first chore of the day—trying to remember all the things from yesterday that ought to be remembered. He heard a noise somewhere in the house and realized that it was only Uncle Darius, who always got up with the sun, putting on the coffeepot for that first cup before Mavis came in. It would be at least another two hours before Athena and Beryl got up.

He lay back down again. If he got up now and went downstairs, Uncle Darius probably would make good the threat about getting him to help with the paste-ups. He wished there were some way he could slip out of the house and go to Rusty's without anybody knowing, but this was unthinkable, because when he came home Athena would raise Cain.

He drifted into sleep again, and when he awoke the second time, Athena was standing over him.

"Patrick, didn't you hear me calling you? It's time to get up. Breakfast is on the table and you're holding everybody up."

Drowsily he got out of bed, wondering why it made any difference if he held everybody up. Beryl was the only one who had to be at a certain place at a certain time. But Athena had a real thing about everybody eating together. In some ways she was as stubborn in her ideas as Uncle Darius, and once he had heard Beryl say to her, "Athena, you're a natural-born old maid." This was after the automobile incident, several years ago, when Beryl had been mad with Athena and Uncle Darius for a long time. Beryl had bought a car, a bright blue convertible, and she hadn't had it more than a few months before Uncle Darius and Athena made her get rid of it. Patrick had never known why they wouldn't let Beryl keep the car, and he had been as mad as she, because he had enjoyed riding in it, especially when Beryl put the top down and went zooming down a country road as though she were competing in a Roman chariot race. But the car had been sold. Beryl hadn't cried or anything, but for a long time she wouldn't speak to Athena or Uncle Darius unless she absolutely had to.

"Are you feeling better this morning, Patrick?" Uncle Darius asked him when he went into the dining room.

"I feel okay," he said.

"Don't say okay," Uncle Darius said. "I think you have enough good words in your vocabulary without having to resort to vulgar slang." And then, to no one in particular, "It's nothing short of a crime, what's happening to the English language these days."

"How are you going to celebrate your first day of freedom, Patrick?" Beryl asked.

"I don't know. Guess I'll go see Rusty."

"If you'd like to invite Rusty to come home and have lunch with you, we'll be glad to have him," Athena said, offering the suggestion as though it were a birthday present.

"I don't know what we'll do," Patrick said. He was hoping maybe Rusty would invite him to stay at the Nichols' for lunch. They always had hot dogs or hamburgers on Saturday and made a picnic out of the meal.

"Just let me know in time to tell Mavis if you decide to bring him," Athena said.

"I'll walk as far as the drugstore with you," Uncle Darius said. "I have to get some things."

They left the house shortly after Beryl and went through the iron gate which opened onto Main Street. Uncle Darius seemed to be in an unusually good mood, and Patrick wondered if he should take advantage of it and ask a few questions. But the questions he wanted to ask might make the mood change, so he walked silently beside his great-uncle and listened to him talk about how much the town had changed since his own childhood.

"It's like living in a different place," Uncle Darius said. "A different world because of all the strangers who've moved here, and they've brought a foreign element which has certainly added nothing to the culture and graciousness of the town. Added money, maybe, and clutter and confusion, but nothing else."

The population of Laurelton had almost doubled in the past ten years, mostly because of the two new plants that had come from Up North. About the time Patrick was born the town had boasted some ten thousand souls; now it was closer to twenty thousand. Main Street, which at one time extended for only eight blocks through the business district, now reached from the northern to the southern limits of the city, and what had once been a comparatively tranquil street with a few stores, offices, and a theater was now a place of almost frantic commerce with new businesses mushrooming from one end to the other.

As they passed the theater, Patrick stopped briefly and looked at the pictures outside. Had it been a good monster show playing, or even a cowboy one, he would have suggested to Rusty that they go. But the pictures showed a bunch of dopey boys and girls mushing it up all over the place, and he wasn't interested. He couldn't understand why anyone would be interested, and that was why it was so hard to try to imagine Athena or Beryl acting the way those girls in the pictures were.

"Come along, Patrick," Uncle Darius said. "I haven't time to speculate on what is showing on the gilded screen."

Out of habit, Uncle Darius almost turned in at the bank when they reached the corner. He hesitated before the glass doors just as one of the doors opened and Father Conroy came out.

The priest smiled at them as though he would like to stop and pass the time of day for a few minutes. "Good morning, Mr. Quincannon. Good morning, Patrick."

"G-good morning," Patrick said uncertainly, knowing that Uncle Darius would not respond and wondering if he himself should be polite and speak or follow Uncle Darius' example.

Uncle Darius pretended he hadn't seen the priest and went on walking, and Father Conroy moved on in the opposite direction.

"Isn't it rude not to speak when you're spoken to?" Patrick asked. He knew immediately that he shouldn't have asked the question. Uncle Darius' good mood had been slaughtered as surely as if Father Conroy had taken an ax to it. His face was beet-red and his nose was twitching, the way it did when he was provoked beyond measure. Patrick decided it would be better to keep a conversation going than to fall into an ominous silence. "I wonder how he knows my name. I never talked to him any, but every time I see him he speaks to me."

"I'd better not hear of your talking to him any," Uncle Darius said.

"Because he's a Catholic?"

Silence.

"Wonder why Catholic ministers dress like that— all black with the funny collar, even in summer."

"Because they like to be different," Uncle Darius said.

"Episcopal ministers dress the same way."

"Episcopalians are nothing but rebel Catholics," Uncle Darius said.

He did not know what Uncle Darius was talking about, but he decided that it would be better to remain in ignorance and find a new topic of conversation.

"I wish we had a car. Uncle Darius, when I'm old enough to learn to drive, do you suppose we could have a car?"

Wrong topic. "We don't need one. We live close enough to everything to walk where we want to go. Besides, walking is healthy, and automobiles lead to nothing but trouble."

"Do you hate them because my grandfather and grandmother were killed in one?"

"Of course not. That was an accident. God's will."

They reached the drugstore and Uncle Darius stopped. "Well, Patrick, have a good time, and call Athena if you decide to bring Rusty home."

"I will. Goodbye, Uncle Darius." He walked faster when he left Uncle Darius, hurrying across the street on a yellow light, and by the time he reached Elmwood Drive, where the Nichols family lived, he was running, head down and elbows in, his spindly legs trying to keep up with his galloping thoughts.

After a strenuous game of war in the Nichols' back yard (Rusty was a Russian general because his name, to him, sounded Russian, and Patrick was Captain Eddie Rickenbacker and flew a plane and got lost in the Pacific), followed by a rest on a stump, during which Patrick told Rusty about his dilemma, Rusty got up from the stump, scrooched up his freckled face in a serious expression, ran his hand through his red hair, and scratched his leg as though a rash had suddenly appeared.

"You know what, Patrick? You got yourself a mess there."

"I hope to tell you," Patrick said.

"Well," Rusty sat down on the stump again, "it's for sure you're not going to find out anything from Miss Athena or Miss Beryl or Uncle Darius. Why don't you hire a detective? One of them private eyes?"

Patrick looked superior. "You know there aren't any privates eyes in Laurelton, and besides, where would I get the money?"

"Then I guess you'll just hafta *be* a detective."

Rusty continued scratching himself thoughtfully. "Do you want me to ask my daddy about it?"

"Great Jehovah, no!" Letting a grownup in on the situation would be the worst possible thing that could happen. He could picture Mr. Nichols going to Uncle Darius (and from what he had heard lately, Uncle Darius was not too happy with Mr. Nichols anyway) and then Uncle Darius seeing that he was in bed by five P.M. daily for a month, with a stomach shrieking from hunger. "I'll have to find out for myself. Do you want to help?"

"Sure," Rusty said. "What do we do first?"

"I don't know," Patrick said. "Rusty, just thinking about it, which would you say would be most likely to be my mother, Athena or Beryl?"

"Jeepers, I don't know. But for your sake I hope it's not Miss Athena. She scars the bejesus outa me."

"Why?"

"I don't know, she just does. Don't she scare you?"

"Sometimes," Patrick admitted.

"Patrick, one thing I don't understand. If Celinda never lived, how come she's buried in your back yard? You said her grave was out there."

"I said her *tombstone* was out there. I explained all that to you."

"I know what you could do." Rusty's face lit up. "You could get one of the gravediggers over at the cemetery to dig her up and see if she's really there."

"That's a crazy-stupid idea. I told you I don't have any money—only my allowance—and I don't think anybody would dig up a coffin for thirty-five cents." But the beginnings of an idea began to form with Rusty's suggestion. He decided to keep it to himself until he had it all thought out and could present a finished plan to Rusty.

"Rus-tee, you out there?" Natalie Nichols' voice broke into their thoughts.

"Yes'm, me and Patrick are playing."

"Lunch is ready. Is Patrick staying?"

"You staying?" Rusty asked.

"Am I invited?"

"Sure, if you want to."

"I'll stay then, but I'll have to call Athena first and tell her."

If Patrick could have had his choice among all the couples he knew in Laurelton, parents of his friends, who could by some miracle become his instant parents, he would have selected Natalie and Louis Nichols. In his estimation, they were real people, not only because they treated him like a thinking, intelligent being, but also because they treated their own kids the same way. He had never heard either of them talk to Rusty the way his family sometimes talked to him, as though he were too dumb-stupid to figure things out for himself. Of course, they weren't quite the same with Elizabeth, Rusty's sister, but she was only three.

Natalie looked a lot like Rusty. She had red hair and a freckled face and was very skinny. She even wore blue jeans around the house a lot, and once he had seen her climbing a tree in the back yard with Rusty. "She reminds me of Lawrence Welk's bubble machine," Beryl said once. "You can't turn her off." Natalie and Beryl were good friends, and Beryl often went to see her, but Natalie almost never went to see Beryl. Patrick supposed that was because they never had much company at the Quincannon house, not the way other people did.

Louis was handsome, in a dark sort of way, and easygoing, and every summer for the past few years he had taken Rusty and Patrick on fishing trips. Elizabeth looked something like her father.

As Patrick knew it would be, the table on the Nichols' back porch was set with paper plates and cups and paper napkins, and there were jars of mustard and relish and chili for the hot dogs. Patrick built his hot dog very carefully, determined not to overlook any of the possibilities, while Natalie haphazardly sloshed things in a roll for Elizabeth.

"Lemonade today, boys, instead of milk," she said. "I thought we'd celebrate with all the trimmings."

"Great," Louis said. "I'll have a double shot— about two fingers."

"You'll get the back of my hand if you aren't careful," Natalie laughed.

"Madam, when are you going to stop beating your husband?" Louis asked.

Patrick looked from one to the other and decided that this, like most of the things they said when they were together, was some sort of private joke. He took an oversized bite on the hot dog, chewed slowly, then asked, as though he were contributing something to a subject which had been under lengthy discussion, "Mrs. Nichols, did you ever see my mother?"

Natalie looked up from her labors on Elizabeth's hot dog and said softly, "No, dear. She died before

I came to Laurelton to live. I lived in Atlanta, you know, until Louis and I were married."

He turned to Louis, about to repeat the question, but Louis said, "How's your Uncle Darius, Patrick?"

"Okay, I guess. He wants me to help him with his paste-ups this summer."

Natalie chuckled and then stopped immediately as though she had been caught laughing at a naughty story. "Is that going to be your project for the summer, Patrick?"

"No'm, he's got another project," Rusty said, and was instantly rewarded with a warning kick under the table from Patrick.

"Do you think your Uncle Darius will ever be talked into selling the Quincannon property, Patrick?" Louis asked.

"No, sir. Not while there's breath in his body."

Now Louis laughed. "Well, I wouldn't want to be quoted on this, but I don't blame him for not selling right now. If he holds out long enough, he'll be offered a better price, and then I don't see how he can refuse."

"He can, though," Patrick said. "I'll bet anything he never sells. Not to a Yankee anyway."

"That place looks downright incongruous to its surroundings," Natalie said. "That old house and jungle right in the middle of town. But in a way, I don't blame Uncle Darius. He'd certainly never feel at home anywhere else. Athena wouldn't either, but Beryl. . . ."

"You think Beryl would like to move?" Louis asked.

"I know she would," Natalie said.

"Uncle Darius and Athena would never leave Laurelton," Patrick said.

"I know, dear." Natalie nodded wisely, then said, "Rusty, have another hot dog. If you and Patrick are going to play soldiers this afternoon, you might as well eat enough for an army."

"I want to look at TV this afternoon," Rusty said. "There's a program. . . ."

"Nothing doing," Natalie said. "You and Patrick are going to play outdoors. We're having guests for dinner, and I don't want either of you underfoot while I'm getting ready. Elizabeth, bite your hot dog from the other end. The dog is running away."

"Mr. Nichols, did you ever see . . ." Patrick began, but Rusty interrupted with, "You'll have old Elizabeth underfoot and besides, Patrick and I won't bother anything."

"Tell you what," Louis said. "You boys be good and stay outside and maybe next week I'll take you up to the lake fishing."

"Which day next week?" Rusty asked.

"We'll decide that after we see how good you are," Louis said.

After lunch Patrick and Rusty went back to their stump. Rusty was ready to marshal his forces for another battle, but Patrick's strategy had been worked out for something different.

"Rusty, I've got an idea. How would you like to come over to my house some night and catch lightning bugs in a blue jar?"

"We can do that here."

"No, I mean we'll pretend to catch lightning bugs. We'll paint some jars and go out back."

"So?"

"So we won't really catch lightning bugs, we'll dig."

"Dig what, fishing worms?"

"Hey, that's not a bad idea. I'll bet we could find a lot and take them with us next week." This was even more plausible than his original idea. Often, without knowing it, Rusty came up with something really good. "That's the most logical thing you've said all day. We wouldn't even have to hide the shovels from them."

"What in tarnation are you talking about?"

"We're going to dig up that grave out back and see who's really buried there."

"You mean *us*, at *night?*"

Patrick pondered this for a minute, then said, "It'd have to be at night. There'd be less chance of Athena or somebody coming to look for us."

"I don't know, Patrick. I never dug up no grave before."

"You scared or something?"

"Course I'm not scared! But I heard they bury people awful deep, and we'd have to dig through practically to China. That would take more'n a night."

"Not with both of us digging like crazy," Patrick said. "You want to?"

"Maybe sometime."

"Tomorrow night," Patrick said. "Tonight's Saturday and Uncle Darius hears my Sunday school lesson, but tomorrow night would be just right. I can tell them we're going to get fishing worms and get the shovels out of the cellar, and they'll never know any better."

"They'll know when they see the hole in the ground."

"After we find what we're looking for we'll throw the dirt back in," Patrick said. "Besides, they hardly ever go back in the woods anyway. You come to my house tomorrow right after supper."

Rusty looked dubious. "We won't be able to see who's in the coffin at night."

"I have a flashlight."

"We-ell, all right. But if you change your mind, you let me know."

"I won't change my mind," Patrick said. "Not in a million years."

Sunday school at Laurelton's First Methodist Church began at 10 A.M. and ended promptly at 10:45. Patrick was always one of the first to leave the church, since he sat near the back of his classroom and hardly waited for the Amen of the dismissal prayer before he bolted. It wasn't that he didn't like Sunday school; it was just that the teacher always talked about things that left a lot of questions in his mind—questions the teacher couldn't come close to answering satisfactorily. She covered her lack of knowledge by saying, "It was God's will, and humans cannot understand the divine."

Patrick couldn't understand it, that was for sure. Why, for instance, if God locked the jaws of the lions and kept them from eating Daniel, didn't He lock the jaws of those lions in Rome that devoured Christians all over the place? And if drinking spirits was bad for you and a sin to boot, why did Jesus turn water into wine for all those people at the wedding? Patrick had long since stopped trying to figure out the why of the Bible. If Uncle Darius couldn't explain it, nobody could. And Uncle Darius' answers hadn't been much better than those of the teacher.

He ambled along the sidewalk on his way home, concentrating on kicking a stone. He had once kicked a stone over eighteen of the small concrete squares before it went into the grass, and ever since, he had tried to break his record. Today it appeared the record would stand.

When he reached the corner of Oak Street and Main, he had to stop his activity in order not to stone the Catholics who were leaving church after ten o'clock Mass. St. Anne's Church, R.C., a small graystone building, was unique among churches in Laurelton in that it did not have a tall white spire. There was a tiny belfry on top of the church like a head on a body that was minus a neck. The Methodists, Baptists, and Presbyterians competed to see which church could have the highest steeple. At the moment the Methodists were ahead, but the Baptists were threatening to renovate again. The Episcopalians weren't in the race, Uncle Darius said, because they considered things like steeples beneath them.

Patrick stopped on the sidewalk and watched the Catholics coming out of church. They paused at the door and shook hands with Father Conroy, just the way the congregation did with Mr. Hancock over at First Methodist. In fact, the Catholics looked pretty much like everybody else, in spite of some of the things Uncle Darius had told him about them. Like burning incense and praying to statues and paying the fare to heaven for dead relatives who, short of funds, had gone to hell.

He would like to look inside that church where so many strange things went on, because he was almost sure that, about Catholics at least, some of Uncle Darius' opinions sprang from misinformation. Uncle Darius had never been inside a Catholic church either, so how could he know for sure what went on?

When the last of the stragglers had shaken hands with the priest and left, Patrick saw Father Conroy go back inside the church. The double doors remained open, so he walked slowly to the three stone steps in front and looked in, but the bright sunlight made the interior appear almost dark. He went cautiously up the steps and found himself in a tiny vestibule, confronted by a wide aisle which led to the altar.

"Why, good morning, Patrick." The voice of Father Conroy, with a tone of surprise unmistakable, boomed at him suddenly, breaking the stillness. The priest materialized beside him like a black genie out of a jar. Patrick jumped and almost cried out. Inadvertently, he took a step backward, wondering what Father Conroy would do to him now that he had been caught in the church.

"I'm glad to see you," Father Conroy said. "But if you came for Mass, you're a bit late." The priest had iron-gray hair and a ruddy complexion and a nose that was about three sizes too large for his face. Patrick could not stop looking at the nose, and neither could he speak.

"Did you come to see me?" Father Conroy asked.

"N-no, sir." He had finally found a very small voice that could not possibly be his. "I—I never saw this church before, inside I mean, so I thought I'd look in."

Father Conroy took him by the hand and led him down the aisle. He did not say a word, and when Patrick looked up into his face, he thought for sure the priest was going to cry, except that grownups, especially ministers, didn't cry.

They stopped at a little railing that separated the altar part of the church from the pews, and Father Conroy went down on one knee and then came right back up again. Patrick watched him for a minute to be sure he wasn't having some kind of attack, and then he looked around him.

Above the altar was a life-size Jesus on the cross —or almost life-size anyway. It scared Patrick to look at the crucifix, because he could even see the nails in the palms of the wooden hands, and the expression on the wooden face was perfectly carved agony.

To the right of the altar was a statue of a man wearing long robes, the kind they wore in pictures in his own Sunday school books. The man had a staff in one hand and held a baby up to his shoulder with the other. On the left of the altar a gleaming white marble lady, also in long robes, had arms outstretched as though she were about to receive someone into them.

"Is that the Virgin Mary?" he whispered to the priest.

Father Conroy nodded. "Yes, Patrick, that is Our Blessed Mother."

Uncle Darius was right about one thing: they did have statues. No, he was right about two things. Patrick's nose crinkled as he tried not to sneeze. There was a pungent odor, not like perfume but sweet, which could have come only from incense.

"Patrick, would you like to stay in here alone for a few minutes and then come to the rectory and ask me questions about anything you don't understand?" Father Conroy asked.

"N-no, thank you," Patrick said quickly. "I've got to be going. Uncle Darius would skin. . . ." He stopped, afraid he might hurt the priest's feelings. He didn't want to do that after Father Conroy had been kind enough to show him the church.

There was a funny sort of half-smile on Father Conroy's face as he said, "Yes, I know. But perhaps someday soon you will come to see me. Do you think you will, Patrick?"

"I—I guess so." He had to get out quick before the priest made him a Catholic. Uncle Darius said they converted folks to Catholic before they even knew what hit them, and certainly he could not go home and announce that he was suddenly a Catholic, because then Uncle Darius really would skin him alive.

They walked slowly back to the door and stopped in the vestibule. "I'm glad you came by, Patrick, and I hope you'll come again. I would like to know you better, and I'd like for you to know the church better."

"Thank you," Patrick said, and edged his way toward the door. "I'll come again—sometime. Goodbye." He almost ran down the steps and out to the sidewalk.

That made three things Uncle Darius was right about. Father Conroy was certainly going to try to turn him into a Catholic, no two ways about it. He was lucky to have escaped this time before the priest hexed all the Methodist out of him. Suddenly he wondered if Father Conroy, like Merlin in the King Arthur stories, had put a spell on him that would cause him to change inside and out. Then he remembered that Catholics *looked* just like everybody else. Uncle Darius would not be able to tell by looking at him that he had been inside the Catholic Church.

The chance to test Uncle Darius came sooner than he expected. Two blocks from home he met his great-uncle striding along the sidewalk on his way to church.

"Well, Patrick, I trust you knew your lesson this morning."

"Yes, sir. I knew it."

"Would you like to go with me to service now?"

"No, thank you. I don't think so."

"You're getting old enough to attend the eleven

o'clock service regularly, but we'll talk about that later."

"Aren't Athena and Beryl going?"

"They elected to stay home this morning. I'll see you later, my boy." And he went on his way, leaving Patrick with the dismal prospect of having to worry about hearing Mr. Hancock's high-pitched, monotonous voice for an hour every Sunday.

He let himself in the iron gate and walked slowly up to the house, hearing the voices of Athena and Beryl through the open living-room window even before he reached the porch. He went to the porch and sat down in the green swing which was suspended from the ceiling by rusted chains. Now he could hear what his aunts were saying.

"Beryl, you are out of your mind," Athena said. "Of course he hasn't been hearing things. The talk in Laurelton died down years ago. The novelty wore off."

"Then why has he suddenly started asking all these questions?" Beryl said. "Mavis said he asked her about both his mother and father."

"I trust Mavis maintained a discreet silence."

"You can trust Mavis, yes," Beryl said.

"I don't like it either," Athena said. "But I'm sure it's simply because he has reached the inquisitive age. He looks around him and is aware that his family situation is somewhat different from that of his friends."

"Is Uncle Darius worried about it?"

"I don't think so," Athena said. "He hasn't said anything, and I think he would have mentioned it if he were worried. After all, we told Patrick from the beginning all that it was feasible for him to know."

Patrick sat as still as a mouse conscious of a cat's presence. He knew that if the swing moved, it would squeak.

"I wish that I had left here years ago," Beryl said, "while I still had the guts to get out. Every time I think about it all, I get depressed all over again."

"You're a fool to let it weigh on your mind after all this time," Athena said. "*I* think about today and tomorrow, not yesterday."

"You and I are different, Athena. You're satisfied to stay here and put up with Uncle Darius' tyranny. I never have been."

"I certainly wouldn't call him a tyrant," Athena said. "He has been good to both of us as well as to Patrick. I don't think you have ever understood him, Beryl. His life can't have been a happy one— not any of it. Brought up by fundamentalist parents who apparently made no secret of the fact that they preferred his twin brother, all of his formative years spent living in his brother's shadow, and then being forced when he might finally have had a life of his own to take on his brother's life and responsibilities. It's a wonder to me that Uncle Darius *isn't* a tyrant. It's a wonder he isn't seething with bitterness. But never one word of complaint from him. Not one word! If he hadn't had duty to home and family and God impressed upon him all his life, if he had been of a less serious-minded nature, we might not have had the comfortable life that we have. You just remember that. Not many uncles would have sacrificed their lives to take care of their nieces and a great-nephew."

"Yes," Patrick heard Beryl sigh, "I'm not denying that. But still, I always hoped there was more to life than this—at least, more to my life."

"If you want to get away so much, why haven't you gone?" Athena asked. "It isn't as though you hadn't had the perfect example set for you."

"You know why I've stayed," Beryl said. "I couldn't leave Patrick."

"Oh?" There was a sarcasm in Athena's voice now. "I suppose you think Uncle Darius and I were incapable of taking care of him."

"Let's not argue about it, Athena. I just didn't *want* to leave him. I *couldn't*."

"Then stop carrying on about your life," Athena said. "It's what you made it. In all of the years Uncle Darius has been with us, he's never expressed regret that *his* life couldn't be different. You certainly have no right, or reason, to complain." There was a pause; then, "I'd better go see if Mavis has everything under control."

Patrick got up and went into the house. "I'm home," he called feebly.

"What took you so long, dear?" Beryl met him at the door. "Did you stop to talk to somebody?"

"Yes." He started upstairs. "I want to put my Sunday school book away."

He closed the door of his room and sat down on the side of his bed. There was little doubt in his mind now about which one was his mother. *You know why I stayed. I couldn't leave Patrick.* When they spoke of Celinda, they said she was like Beryl. Of course she was like Beryl; she *was* Beryl. He should have known all the time that it could never in a million years have been Athena.

He got up and went to the window seat, looking out across the green thicket that served as a back yard. Tonight he would know for sure. He and Rusty would dig up the coffin and. . . .

A sudden thought caused him to panic. Coffins were locked, or at least shut up so tight that he and Rusty probably could not look inside. And what if the coffin were in one of those vault things that he had seen advertised in the newspaper by Mr. Freeling's Funeral Parlor? They'd never get into one of those.

So what was the point in digging? There was no clear answer, but he knew he was going to dig up that grave anyway. Somehow there had to be an answer to *something*.

Later, he heard Uncle Darius come in, and he started downstairs, knowing that dinner would be announced almost immediately. He stopped when he heard Beryl say, "Why that perturbed expression, Uncle Darius? Didn't Mr. Hancock astound you with his usual eloquence?"

"The sermon was middling good," Uncle Darius said. "His text was 'Blessed are they that mourn, for they shall be comforted.'"

"I'm sure it was inspiring," Athena said, as though she was sure of no such thing. "Dinner is ready. Shall I call Patrick?"

"No, not yet," Uncle Darius said. "I want to take a little walk first."

Patrick heard him go through the house and then heard the screen door of the back porch slam. He went back to his room and looked out the window. Uncle Darius stood on the back steps for a minute, looking around him as though he had never seen his surroundings before. Then he walked slowly toward the trees and disappeared into the woods, almost as though he had been swallowed by man-eating plants.

For the first time in his whole, entire life, Patrick felt sorry for Uncle Darius. It had never occurred to him before that Uncle Darius was a person for whom one should work up any sympathy, but listening to Athena had given him some new thoughts about his great-uncle, and there was something about the way he had gone into the woods—shoulders sagging, his walk slow—that made Patrick sad. For the first time, Patrick thought of him as a person and not just as Uncle Darius, and although he wasn't quite sure why, it saddened him.

He went downstairs and passed through the kitchen, ignoring Mavis' question, "You about ready to eat, Patrick?" and went outside to the door to the cellar. In the cellar, after much scrambling through suffocating dust and debris, he found two shovels, took them outside, and put them under the back steps. Just as he started in the house, he saw Uncle Darius returning.

He was still walking as though he were Methuselah's grandfather, and when he spoke his voice sounded soft and feeble. "Why aren't you getting ready for dinner, Patrick? You know we don't like to be kept waiting."

For a minute Patrick thought he saw tears in

Uncle Darius' eyes, but of course that couldn't be. This seemed to be his day for seeing non-existent tears.

"I'm ready," he said. "I've just got to wash my hands, is all."

Uncle Darius did not reply. His head seemed to go down even lower, and Patrick knew suddenly that his walk in the woods, a place he almost never went, had been to Celinda's grave.

# 5

If the atmosphere at Sunday dinner had seemed strangely quiet and strained (usually Uncle Darius started by expounding on Mr. Hancock's sermon and ended by preaching one of his own), it was even worse at supper. Or perhaps Patrick only thought it was worse because he was beginning to get an acute case of fidgets, brought on by thinking about the work to be done that night.

"May I be excused?" Patrick asked, swallowing the last of his cream cheese and pineapple sandwich. (Mavis did not come back on Sunday nights, and Athena made sandwiches and they ate in the kitchen.)

"Not until the rest of us have finished," Athena said in a tone which told Patrick he should have known better than to ask.

"What's the big hurry?" Beryl asked. "You've

been acting like the bird that swallowed the cat all day."

"Beryl, it's not the bird that . . ." Uncle Darius began.

"I know," she laughed. "But it makes more sense to me that way."

"You should try to be correct, even when using platitudes and clichés," Uncle Darius said.

"Getting back to the point," Athena said, "what *is* wrong with you, Patrick? Why did you stay in your room all afternoon?"

"I was reading."

"Something suitable for the Sabbath, I hope," Uncle Darius said. The comment did not call for an answer.

"Are you in a hurry to get back to your book?" Beryl asked.

"No, Rusty is coming over. We're going to dig worms."

"Dig *worms!*" Athena's face knotted itself up into an expression of extreme disgust.

"Yes, ma'am, fishing worms," Patrick said calmly. "Rusty's daddy is going to take us fishing."

"But it will be dark soon," Athena said. "You can't go out digging at night."

"Night's the best time to dig for fishing worms," Patrick said. He wasn't sure about the accuracy of the statement, but it sounded good.

"What are you going to do with the worms after you dig them?" Beryl asked.

"Put them in a bucket and keep them until we go fishing." He thought he saw now the reason for their concern. "Don't worry, I wasn't figuring on bringing them in the house."

"Where are you going to dig?" Beryl asked.

He pointed. "Out back."

Uncle Darius straightened in the hard kitchen chair. "I find this discussion of worms completely out of place at the table," he said.

"Be thankful we're not eating macaroni," Beryl said.

Uncle Darius scowled at her. She was saved from reproval by the sudden entrance of Rusty.

"Good evening," he said. "You still want to do it, Patrick?"

Athena jerked around, startled by the intrusion. "Did you ring the bell, Rusty?"

"No'm, I hollered to Patrick from the porch, but I guess he didn't hear me. Patrick, you still . . ."

"May I be excused now?" Patrick interrupted quickly.

"Yes, go ahead," Athena said. "But don't stay out there too long."

"It might take a while," Patrick said, "to find enough of them for fishing. Sometimes the fish eat them off the hook before you even know it, so it takes a lot."

"Patrick!" This from Uncle Darius.

"Yes, sir, I didn't say it. You go on out back, Rusty, while I get my flashlight."

"I'll wait for you here," Rusty said. He seemed able to keep his enthusiasm for the venture within bounds.

Patrick took the stairs two at a time, grabbed the flashlight from his bedside table, and raced back to the kitchen. He didn't want to give Rusty a chance to open his big yap about what they were going to do.

They walked quickly across the small grassy clearing beyond the back porch, but their steps slowed as they reached the trees.

"Patrick, you sure this is a good idea?" Rusty asked.

"You got a better one?"

"I reckon not." Rusty sighed in resignation. "How we going to know how far to dig?"

"I borrowed Athena's tape measure." He pulled the yellow tape from his pocket. "We only have to go six feet down. That's how deep they bury folks."

"That's deeper than we are," Rusty said. "How we going to get out of the hole?"

"That's easy enough," Patrick said. "When you're in a dirt hole all you have to do is dig steps in the side and climb up."

"I got on my Sunday clothes," Rusty said practically.

"What in tarnation for?"

"Because it's Sunday, and Mama said if I was going to your house I had to wear them."

"Well, I guess we can brush the dirt off you before you go home."

They continued their walk in silence, each concentrating on picking his way through the thick growth of weeds and underbrush. When they reached the point where the trees thinned out, they saw the sun, a great red burst of flame, sinking at an almost visible rate.

"Patrick, you sure we couldn't do this in the daytime?" Rusty asked.

"I explained that to you," Patrick said with great patience, even as his own heart beat faster. "This is the only time. There's the grave over there." He pointed to the white marble tombstone which had taken on a pinkish hue in the sunset.

Rusty went up to it and read slowly, "Celinda, beloved daughter of Donald and Sarah Quincannon. What's that other stuff written on there, Patrick?"

"Some sort of foreign language."

"Was your mother a foreigner?"

Patrick ignored the question while he studied the ground, trying to decide where to start digging. He picked up a stick, paced off what he thought was six feet from the stone, and put the stick down.

"We'll start near the stone and work our way down to the stick," he said.

The ground around the stone was covered with soft, velvety moss, and the first few shovelfuls came up easily. "Get the moss in big chunks, Rusty, so we can put it back on top after we fill up the hole again."

They had been digging for only a few minutes when Rusty said, "My hands are getting sore." He put the shovel down and looked at his hands. "They're red, too."

"You'll get used to it after a while. Just keep digging." Now that the moss was up, the earth was harder, and each time the shovel came up there was less dirt in it.

"Patrick, I don't think I like this. Mama told me not to stay long, so I guess I'd better go."

"Rusty Nichols, if you chicken out on me now I'll never speak to you again. And I won't go with you and your daddy on any more old fishing trips. I'll tell everybody I know what a baby you are, and I'll tell them you still wet the bed."

Rusty continued digging.

They were not progressing nearly as fast as Patrick had thought they would. The sun was down now and the darkness was beginning to settle over them like a blanket. Although the hole didn't look very deep, there seemed to be enough dirt on the pile where they were throwing it to fill three holes of the same size.

Patrick took out the tape measure and put it in the hole. Not quite two feet deep and not as long as it was deep.

"Maybe she's buried on the other side of the tombstone," Rusty said helpfully.

"She's buried on *this* side, where the writing is," Patrick said. He picked up the shovel, which now weighed a good ten pounds more than it had when he began digging, and resumed his work.

"My hand has got a blister on it," Rusty said. "It hurts."

"It'll all be gone by the time you face your Maker," Patrick said, quoting Uncle Darius.

It was now completely dark, except for a few stringy rays of moonlight which couldn't quite get through the trees to light the ground.

"This'll help." Patrick turned on the flashlight

and placed it on the tombstone at an angle so it would shine on their labors.

They dug in silence for what seemed a very long time, the only sound being an occasional grunt as one of them struggled to push his shovel down into the resisting dirt. Finally, Patrick said, "Okay, I guess we better rest for a minute." He dropped his shovel and sat down, leaning against the tombstone. Rusty squatted on his haunches, inspecting the hole.

"It'll take us all night tonight, and all tomorrow night, and the night after that to get to that coffin, Patrick."

"We got to finish tonight."

Rusty sighed. "I wonder what Mama and Daddy and old Elizabeth are doing now?" He made the statement as one who has been away from home for a long, long time.

"I *know* what they're doing in my house," Patrick said. "Beryl is watching TV, and Athena and Uncle Darius are reading or talking."

"Maybe Miss Beryl is meeting her boy friend," Rusty said.

"*Beryl?* She hasn't got a boy friend."

"That's all you know. She has, too."

"Don't be dumb-stupid," Patrick said. "Beryl never had a boy friend in. . . ." He stopped, remembering. At some time in her life she certainly must have had a boy friend, or *he* wouldn't be here now. "What makes you think she has a boy friend?"

"I don't think, I *know*. Only I'm not supposed to say anything about it, not even to you."

"Why not?"

"Because your Uncle Darius would have a fit or something if he found out. Mama said so."

"If you know so much, who is it?"

Rusty was silent.

"It isn't anybody, that's why you can't tell me." He waited but this brought no response either. "If you don't tell me, Rusty, I'm going to tell everybody that you. . . ."

"It's no use, telling me what you're going to do, Patrick Tolson," Rusty said, his voice high and quivery. "I promised my mama, and I'm not going to tell you anything."

"No boy friends have ever come to see Beryl," Patrick said.

"Course not. I reckon they're scared of Uncle Darius."

"Then where does she see a boy friend?"

"At . . . I'm not going to tell you." Rusty got up and started digging furiously. "And pretty soon I'm going home. I don't want to look inside any old coffin anyway."

Patrick took out the tape measure. Almost three and a half feet now. Another hour or two. . . .

"Pat-rick. Patrick, you all come in now." The voice of Athena came through the trees like a ghost hallooing from the Beyond.

"Oh, my gosh," Patrick said. "What'll we do now?"

"We can finish tomorrow," Rusty said. "I'll help you in the morning."

Patrick said nothing. He knew the job had to be finished tonight. Tomorrow, Uncle Darius might take it in his head to visit the grave again.

"I'll leave my shovel here," he said. "You can put yours under the back steps and I'll put it away tomorrow."

Athena was waiting for them in the kitchen. "Rusty, your mother called and . . . My Lord, look at you! Both of you!"

The boys looked down at their clothes self-consciously. "I guess we got a little dirt on us," Patrick said unnecessarily.

"I trust you found enough worms to take care of a whole summer of fishing," Athena said. "Rusty, Natalie called and said for you to come home. And Patrick, it's past your bedtime, too. Be sure you get a bath first, though."

"Yes, ma'am. I'll see you tomorrow, Rusty."

"Do you want me to . . ." Rusty began, but Patrick interrupted. "I'll probably bring the worms to your house."

After Rusty left, Patrick went upstairs and ran water in the tub, but he did not get in. He stayed long enough for Athena to think he was bathing, then he put on his pajamas and went to the head of the stairs. He could hear them talking in the living room, and it sounded as though it would be hours before they ran out of conversation and decided to go to bed. He went back to his room and humped up his pillow under the sheet, then he crept silently downstairs and through the back hall to the kitchen. The screen door squeaked a little as he opened it, but the voices flowed on.

With his flashlight giving a thin, yellow stream of light, he went back through the woods. Everything looked different now. The trees were like giants hovering around him, ready to reach out and grab him. He walked faster, stumbling several times before he reached the scene of his and Rusty's work.

He had never been so scared in his whole, entire life, but he didn't have time to think about that now. He had to finish what he had started. He arranged the flashlight on the tombstone again and picked up the shovel. The way the light was shining, it showed up the word CELINDA, making it look large and grotesque. He looked away from the stone and began digging, ignoring, along with his fear, the ache in his back and his throbbing hands.

For a long time he dug, breathing in tempo with the motion of pulling out the shovel. When his breath came fast, he knew he had to stop and rest. But the shovel had struck something solid, so he dug more frantically than ever.

It was only a rock, a big one that took all of his strength to move. That out of the way, he continued for a few minutes more before he sat down and wiped his gritty hand across his forehead.

It must be awfully late now, maybe after midnight. He measured again and the hole was four and a half feet deep, but it wasn't very long and he knew that after he got to the coffin, he'd have to make the hole as long as it was deep. He could worry about that later.

The hole was already as deep as he was tall, and he was having trouble throwing the dirt out. Besides, he was working in almost total darkness because the beam of the flashlight went over the top of the hole.

He dug steadily for a few minutes more and then put down the shovel and sat down, leaning against the cool, dank earth.

When he opened his eyes, he started, not knowing at first where he was. Then, when he knew, he had a feeling of strangeness. Something was different. The sky above him, which was all he could see from the depths of the hole, was no longer black but gray. He crawled up the sloping side of the hole and looked around him. It was so late that it was almost morning. He had no idea how long he had slept.

His thin body felt cramped, and he ached all over. In about an hour, he figured, the sun would be up, and he still hadn't finished his work. The hole now measured five feet. One foot to go, and it was now or never.

He grabbed the shovel and pitched in as though all the demons of hell were after him—or he after them. In a short while he had reached the six-foot mark, but he had not come to the coffin. He kept digging.

The gray sky above him turned pink, and he knew he would have to go back to the house and slip into his room, because it was almost time for Uncle Darius to go downstairs for his first cup of coffee.

But just a little bit more . . . a bit deeper. He forced his hands, which now felt scalded, to hold the shovel, push into the earth, pull up, and throw the dirt over the slope.

And then he stopped.

He had dug a little over seven feet—and there was no coffin.

He climbed out of the hole, dragging the shovel with him. He would have to come back later in the day and put that big mound of dirt back in the hole. Maybe Rusty would help him.

He walked through the woods slowly, still dragging the shovel, and he felt hot tears stinging his eyes and washing small paths down his grit-encrusted cheeks. He wiped his nose on the sleeve of his pajamas and kicked at the trunk of a tree with his bare foot.

He was being the biggest, silliest baby in the whole, entire world to cry, because he had known from the beginning that he would not find Celinda. He had known all the time that they had lied to him. There was no Celinda, and never had been.

# 6

It wasn't an unusual awakening; in fact, it was very usual. Athena was standing over him saying, "Patrick, didn't you hear me call you? Get up now, you're holding everybody up."

He opened his eyes, but it was a long time before they would focus on the wiry, reddish hair, the snapping blue eyes, and the expression that said clearly, "Go to the ant, thou sluggard."

He had not been asleep more than an hour or two. He figured this out as soon as he awoke. To Athena it was just another Monday morning. To him, it was the morning after he had been digging all night. He pulled the sheet up around his neck, afraid she would see how dirty he was.

"I'll be ready in a little while," he said. "I think I'll take a bath."

"You had a bath before you went to bed last night," she said. "Hurry up and get dressed and come to breakfast."

She left him and he turned over in bed, wishing he could sleep the day through. But he knew he couldn't. There was a game to be played downstairs—pretending that everything was as it always was—and then work to be done out back.

Slowly he got out of bed and went to the bathroom. He was appalled at his appearance in the mirror in the medicine cabinet. His face was streaked with dirt, and he wondered why Athena had not commented. He took a bird bath, sponging himself and hoping that he would pass inspection. But there was nothing he could do about his hands. They were raw, blistered, and blood-red.

He dressed quickly and went downstairs, hoping that this would not be a conversational breakfast. They were all at the table and looked at him as he entered.

"Did you have a successful evening with your big game hunting, Patrick?" Beryl asked as he sat down.

"Not very," he said, and at the same time Uncle

Darius said, "Let's not start that again, please, Beryl."

Patrick looked at his hands in his lap and he knew he could not show them above the table. They would know he had been digging more than worms. "May I please be excused?" he asked. "I don't want any breakfast."

"Are you ill, Patrick?" Athena asked.

"No, I'm just not hungry."

"Unless you are ill, you will eat your breakfast," Athena said.

"I told you something was the matter with the boy," Uncle Darius said. "He hasn't been himself for several days."

"Growing pains, Mavis says," Athena said.

He tuned them out and concentrated on his oatmeal, keeping the palm of his right hand balled up around the spoon and his left hand in his lap. No matter how much his hands hurt, he would have to go back out there this morning and shovel the dirt back in the hole, then fit the pieces of moss over the dirt—like putting together a jigsaw puzzle.

"What big things are you and Rusty planning for today?" Beryl asked.

Before he could answer, Uncle Darius said, "Patrick is going to help me with my paste-ups this morning."

"But I told Rusty . . ." Patrick began.

"You may play with Rusty this afternoon if you'd like," Uncle Darius said. "This morning you are helping me."

"Yes, sir." He looked down at the lumpy mound

of oatmeal and thought about the mound of dirt waiting for him. But there was no point in arguing, begging, or cajoling. Once Uncle Darius made up his mind. . . .

The phone rang, and Mavis answered in the kitchen. She appeared at the door a minute later and said, "Mr. Darius, a Mr. Christopher Danton wants to know if he can talk to you today about some land."

"Christopher Danton?" Athena said. "Is he the one . . . ?

"He owns the Empire Textile Mills," Uncle Darius said. "He's the Yankee who's trying to steal our birthright. Tell him, Mavis, that I expect to be busy all day. I can't see him."

Mavis disappeared and then returned almost immediately. "He says how about tonight. He can come by after dinner."

Uncle Darius sighed. "All right, tell him I can give him a few minutes of my time tonight. I might as well see him and get this over with once and for all. I don't want that man pestering me any more."

"Maybe he's going to up the offer again," Beryl said.

"I'm sure he is," Uncle Darius said, "or he wouldn't bother to come."

Patrick did not look up from his oatmeal. His mind was going round and round with unanswered questions, questions he could never ask Uncle Darius.

Uncle Darius had said that not while the earthly remains of one Quincannon lay buried out back would he sell the land. But there were no remains of *anybody* buried out back. There was nothing but the deep, empty hole Patrick had dug last night. Uncle Darius knew there was no one buried there. He knew there was no such person as Celinda.

Why had Uncle Darius put up a tombstone for a Quincannon (even a mythical Quincannon) in a place where no other Quincannons were buried? Donald and Sarah Quincannon rested in the Laurelton cemetery.

"The thing I can't understand," Uncle Darius was saying, "is why Louis Nichols went to work for those Yankees. I always thought he had better sense."

"It's a good job," Beryl said. "Manager of the plant. It pays about twice as much as the job he had before the mills opened here."

"Money isn't everything," Uncle Darius said, and Athena nodded solemnly.

After Beryl had left for the shop, Uncle Darius called Patrick into the library. "Now, my boy, sit down and I'll show you how it's done." He had yesterday's newspaper in his hands. On the desk in front of him was the current scrapbook. "I'll select and clip the news stories, and you can paste them in. And at the top of each page, you are to write the date. Here, you can use my pen. I hope, Patrick, that after I am gone, you will continue this project. It is very worthwhile."

"Yes, sir," Patrick agreed, but he made no promise. Somehow he could not visualize himself spending his life pasting newspaper articles in a scrapbook.

"After you have worked with me long enough, you'll be able to tell which stories are worth saving and which are nothing more than black type used to fill a white space. Now then, we'll get started."

Patrick worked automatically, putting paste at the corners of the clippings Uncle Darius gave him and sticking them into the book.

"Your mind is not on what you're doing, Patrick," Uncle Darius said. "You must always concentrate on the job at hand. Look at that last clipping. It's on the page crooked. Take it up before the paste dries and put it in straight."

He did as he was told and tried harder to keep his mind on the job at hand, but his thoughts kept going back to the job that had to be done out back.

It did not take long, because Uncle Darius decided that not too many history-making events had happened in the world the day before. When they finished, he said, "I am going downtown now, Patrick. Would you like to walk with me?"

"No, sir. Thank you. I told Rusty. . . ." His voice trailed off as he tried to remember what he had told Rusty.

"Very well. I shall see you at lunch."

This gave Patrick an idea of how he could stay out all day without having the others check on him. "I may eat lunch at Rusty's," he said.

"You ate there Saturday," Uncle Darius said. "You will wear out your welcome."

"I'll just eat today, then I won't go again for a long time," Patrick said.

"You'd better ask Athena first." Uncle Darius picked up his hat and cane and left the house, humming softly. Patrick waited until he had passed through the iron gate, then he himself left quickly, going out the front door so Athena and Mavis would not see him. They would think he was with Uncle Darius.

He went to the back of the house and got one of the shovels from under the steps, then proceeded along the now well-known path through the woods.

In bright daylight the grave, or what was supposed to be a grave, looked quite different. The indefinable fear which had possessed him last night was gone, and as he looked at the deep hole he had dug and the high pile of dirt beside it, he thought for the first time that there was something pathetic about a grave with a tombstone where no one was buried.

All of his life Celinda had existed for him as the beautiful angel Mavis had described. He loved Uncle Darius and Athena and Beryl and Mavis, but Celinda had been somebody special for him. She had been perfection which would never be marred or become less than perfect. To find out now that that perfection had never existed was the same as finding out there was no God.

He wondered about that for a minute. Was God also somebody who was dreamed up by Uncle Darius and his aunts? Was God somebody they used to threaten him with when he was bad or to give him a reward when he was good?

But no, that couldn't be, because everybody in Laurelton believed in God. Even the Catholics.

Did everybody in Laurelton believe in Celinda? He supposed that didn't matter much now that *he* knew the truth. The thing was, he was going to have to stop thinking of Celinda as his mother. He was going to have to stop thinking about Celinda at all. How long would it take to get used to the idea that Beryl was really his mother? Even though he knew now, he still could not quite take it in.

He worked as fast as he could with his hands hurting the way they were. Holding the shovel was agony, but at least it was easier to throw dirt back in the hole than it had been to get it out, and the work went much faster. If he hurried, he might even be able to finish in time for lunch.

Every now and then he paused and looked at the tombstone. *Requiescat in pace*. Sometime he would have to ask what that meant. It would be a big joke on him if it meant "Nobody Buried Here." All that digging for nothing.

He was tired. He was so tired and sleepy that he thought he'd like to fall right down in the hole (or what was left of it) and sleep forever. In fact, he might be asleep on his feet right now, except that when you were asleep you did not feel pain, and he was acutely conscious of the pain in his hands. He worked faster, because the sooner he finished, the sooner he could go soak his hands in cold water. They were on fire.

Finally, the hole was filled, and he started in amazement. There was almost as much dirt left over as he had thrown back into the hole. How could that be? He beat the dirt down with his shovel, but there was no way to get it all back in the hole.

He got down on his knees and methodically began to place the clumps of moss over the dirt. They didn't fit right either, but he did the best he could. Then he looked around for a way to dispose of the surplus dirt. The only thing he could think of was to sling it out around the trees and hope that nobody would notice. He also hoped that nobody would come walking through the woods anytime soon, because the grave certainly did not look the way it had before he dug it up.

He took his shovel and went back to the house, got the other shovel from beneath the steps and replaced them both in the cellar. Then he went in the house, using the front door again, and crept upstairs to the bathroom, where he held his hands under the cold water faucet for a long time. It was nearly two-thirty, so lunch was over and Beryl had gone back to the shop. There was no sound from downstairs. He imagined Uncle Darius was napping in his big chair in the library, and Athena was probably in the living room reading or knitting.

He went to his room and fell across the bed, holding the blistered palms of his hands up and away from him as though they were alien objects, and he was asleep instantly.

The voices seeped into his consciousness slowly, and he awoke slowly, fighting off wakefulness the way he sometimes fought off sleep. But the voices were persistent, and finally he sat up and listened. It was dark in his room and dark outside, and it was a long time before he knew what day it was and why he was in bed with his clothes on.

"But he said he was going to Rusty's," Uncle

Darius said. "He said he was going to eat lunch there."

"I called Natalie," Athena said, "and she said they hadn't seen Patrick all day. Something has happened to him. I just know it. He's never gone off without telling me. If he were all right, he would have been here for supper."

"And where did he eat lunch?" Beryl asked. "I think we should call the police."

Patrick was suddenly aware of a gnawing hunger that was like sickness. He felt weak. He hadn't had anything to eat since that scroungy old oatmeal at breakfast and he hadn't really eaten that.

He got up and went downstairs. "Is supper over?"

Three pairs of eyes focused on him as though they were seeing something unreal.

"Patrick!" Beryl was the first to find her voice. "Where in heaven's name have you been?"

It was a minute before he could think of an answer. "I was taking a nap."

"All day?" Athena's incredulity registered clearly.

"I—I guess so. I was pretty tired."

They continued to stare at him. Then Uncle Darius said, "I told you the boy wasn't well. I think we should call Dr. Armbruster."

"I'm okay," Patrick said. "But I'm hungry."

Suddenly Beryl laughed. "Come on, sweetie, I'll find you something to eat. My Lord, I would never have thought of looking for you *in your room*, of all places."

"After pulling a stunt like that, he should be sent to bed without his supper," Athena said.

"Apparently he's been without two meals and has had enough of bed," said Beryl.

She took him to the kitchen and gave him a glass of milk and some cold chicken and biscuits that were left from supper. He ate greedily, without talking, and Beryl watched him in silence. When they returned to the living room, Athena and Uncle Darius were still discussing whether Dr. Armbruster should be called. Finally, Uncle Darius said, "We'll wait until morning and see how he is then. It's about time for that Yankee to get here, and I wouldn't want Frank Armbruster to come in and find me entertaining Yankees."

Beryl looked at her watch and said, "I'd better go outside. Natalie is picking me up." A horn sounded from the street as she spoke.

Patrick followed Beryl to the porch and decided to walk with her to the gate. "Are you going to see the Nichols?"

"Yes."

"Tell Rusty I couldn't make it today. I'll see him tomorrow maybe."

"I'll tell him." Beryl went out to the street and got into the car beside Natalie.

It suddenly occurred to Patrick that maybe Natalie was taking Beryl to meet her boy friend. Maybe all of those evenings when Beryl was supposed to be visiting the Nichols she was really meeting someone else. Natalie, of course, was helping her, and that was how Rusty had known that Beryl had a boy friend.

He walked slowly back to the house, unconsciously kicking at loose gravel along the narrow walk.

Shortly after Beryl left, the man came to talk to Uncle Darius about selling the property to Empire Textile Mills. Patrick was standing in the hall when he arrived. He was very tall and had dark hair and talked in a funny way, not at all like the people in Laurelton. Patrick supposed this was because he was a Yankee and didn't know any better. Maybe after he had been in Laurelton for a while, he would talk like everybody else.

He shook hands solemnly with Patrick when Uncle Darius introduced them and said, "I've heard quite a lot about you, Patrick," and Patrick decided this must be a big lie, because where could Mr. Danton have heard about him? Certainly not from Uncle Darius, who was the only one in the family he had talked to before.

Patrick sat on the stairs, hoping he would hear something of the conversation going on in the library, but Athena had the TV on in the living room, and most of what he got was a combination of voices from the two rooms. He did hear Uncle Darius say, "Your offer, Mr. Danton, as far as I'm concerned, is no more to the point than the last one. My nieces and I own this property together, and we are agreed that it will remain in the family."

"Eighty-five thousand is our last offer, Mr. Quincannon," the man said. "We don't feel the land is worth more than that, especially when we can buy five acres near the city limits. That location isn't as convenient for an office building, but we can get it for much less, and in a few years the business district will have reached that point. I think you'd better. . . ."

And then the sound on television got louder for a commercial, and Patrick couldn't hear any more from the library.

He went to his room and undressed, but having slept all afternoon, he was not sleepy now. In a few minutes he heard Uncle Darius show the man to the front door. And later still, after he had turned on his bed lamp and started reading a Hardy Boys, he heard Uncle Darius and Athena come upstairs and go to their rooms.

He read for a long time, and when he turned off his light, he found he still was not sleepy and just lay in bed thinking and thinking.

It must have been very late when he finally went to sleep, but he still had not heard Beryl come in.

# 7

Patrick spent the next few days studying—not books, but the people around him—and before he finished, he decided that he understood books, even arithmetic, better. There was no way to explain Uncle Darius. He was just Uncle Darius and that was all there was to it. And Athena was Athena and Beryl was. . . . Well, it was hard to say that Beryl was Beryl, because sometimes Beryl was one

way and sometimes another. She could be the Beryl who was Uncle Darius' niece and Athena's sister and act so that anybody would know she was kin to them. Or she could be the Beryl who was his pal and sometimes his ally against the other two. Like the times when she seemed to be teasing Uncle Darius about something, knowing full well that Uncle Darius was a person you couldn't tease.

It still came hard to him, trying to think of Beryl as his mother, although there was no longer any doubt about it. She just didn't seem quite *motherly*. Unless, of course, she was a mother like Natalie Nichols who was a lot of fun and almost never scolded Rusty and Elizabeth.

Athena was really the one who bossed him around and told him what to do and what not to do. She was, to his way of thinking, more the mother type, but it was even harder to think of her as a mother than it was Beryl. The reason was, of course, that he could never in a trillion years imagine Athena doing that thing that would have produced him, while Beryl. . . . He just didn't know.

The week passed slowly. He stayed close to home most of the time and did not even see Rusty. He thought about the proposed fishing trip, but since he did not hear from Rusty, he supposed the trip had been called off or postponed because Mr. Nichols was too busy to take them.

He spent the mornings helping Uncle Darius with the paste-ups and the afternoons in the swing on the front porch reading. Several times Athena came out to the porch and said, "Patrick, for heaven's sake, are you still sitting here? Go out in the sunshine and play. You'll never get any sun sitting here, and if you stay so milk-white all summer Uncle Darius will be convinced you're anemic."

"I will when I finish this chapter," he would say, but he could never think of anything to play. He guessed he just wasn't in a playing mood.

"I'm not sure reading all those mystery books is good for you anyway," Athena went on. "Your imagination is already overdeveloped."

"Yes'm." And his eyes never left the page. The books were only a way to pass the time and to get his mind off the mystery that his own life had become. Maybe when he was grown-up and in high school they would think he was old enough to tell him what was what. But that was another four or five years away, and he couldn't wait that long.

By Friday afternoon he had another plan. Mavis, as he had thought from the beginning, would come nearer telling him the truth than the others. But she would never say one word while she was in the Quincannon house that would displease Uncle Darius. He knew this for sure. So the only thing to do was to go to see Mavis at her house.

He waited until she had finished the lunch dishes and started home before he called to Athena, "I'm going to see what's on at the movies," and then he followed Mavis.

He stayed far enough behind her so that she wouldn't see him and send him home. When he was a little kid, Mavis had taken him home with her often for an afternoon when Athena was going out to a meeting of her church circle or book club, but it had been a long time since he had been to see Mavis. Usually Tom, her husband, was there, because he didn't work steady. Mavis said he had the high blood and couldn't work all the time, so Tom did yard work and odd jobs when his blood wasn't high. Patrick had heard Athena say that it wasn't Tom's blood that was high most of the time, but Tom had looked pretty sick some of the times Patrick had seen him, so he thought Athena must be wrong.

Beyond the business district, Mavis turned on Vine Street and walked toward the colored section of town. Her home, a small neat frame house which looked as though it had been freshly painted a vivid blue, was the first house beyond the lot where the school buses were parked during the summer. Patrick gave a grunt of distaste as he looked at the three rows of orange buses with LAURELTON PUBLIC SCHOOLS painted in big black letters on the sides.

He walked faster. Now that Mavis was home, it was all right if he caught up with her.

As she was unlocking her front door he went up to her, and not knowing exactly what to say, he spoke as though he had not seen her all day. "Hullo, Mavis."

She wheeled around. "Patrick! Lord have mercy, what are you doing here?"

"I decided to come to see you, since I didn't have anything else to do." This didn't sound exactly right to him, but if there was anything wrong with the statement, Mavis apparently didn't notice.

"Miss Athena know where you are? You like to have scared us all to death last week, Patrick."

"I told her I was going out for a little while." He hoped fervently that Tom was not at home, because he could talk to Mavis better without Tom moping around the house nursing his high blood.

"Tom's cutting the grass over at the Ainsleys today," Mavis said, as if she had heard him hoping. "Well, now that you're here, you might as well come in for a spell."

He followed her into the small living room, which was just as he remembered it. There was a brown sofa which sagged at one end because the springs were broken; there were assorted chairs of assorted colors; there was a funny looking bureau that had a mirror in a gold frame over it; and on the wall above the sofa there was a big picture of Jesus, showing only His head and shoulders. Jesus had on a red robe that clashed with His rust-colored hair, and the yellow halo clashed with the hair also. But all in all, it was a nice picture because Jesus had such a nice face. Usually Patrick didn't like beards, but the beard kind of went with Jesus, and he couldn't imagine Him without one. And he knew for a fact that Jesus was so busy going around preaching and making miracles that He never had time to shave anyway.

"Sit down, Patrick," Mavis said. "You want some ice cream? I got some here, and I don't reckon Miss Athena'd mind if you had some." She seemed to be trying to think of a way to entertain her unexpected guest.

"That would be right tasty," he said solemnly, wondering how to begin his discussion with her.

He thought about it while she went to the kitchen to get the ice cream.

"Mavis," he said hesitantly when she returned and gave him the ice cream in a dish as blue as her house, "tell me about my mother."

She looked surprised. "Lord, Patrick, are you going to start that again? All of us have told you about Miss Cee over and over again."

"I'm not talking about any Celinda," he said. "I said tell me about my mother."

She looked at him uncomprehendingly and he knew he was going to get nowhere that way.

"Did you go to her funeral?" he asked.

"No, I didn't go," she said. "I was too broke up. I thought they'd have to bury me, too. Besides, I had to take care of you."

"I guess all the others went."

"Well, Miss Athena and Miss Beryl did, but Mr. Darius stayed home."

"Why didn't he go?"

"Because he said he wouldn't put foot . . . I expect he was too broke up to."

Patrick finished the ice cream and put the dish down on the three-legged table by the sofa. "Mavis, you know good and well there never was any funeral."

"What you talking about, Patrick? Of course there was a funeral. You don't think they'd just put Miss Cee in the ground like she was some heathen, do you?"

"They never put her in the ground at all," Patrick said. "You know as well as I do that there's not one living soul buried out there where that tombstone is."

Mavis gasped. "Jesus God, Patrick!" Then she was quiet for so long that Patrick was afraid she wasn't going to talk to him any more. Finally, she said, "How you know there's nobody buried there?"

"Because I do, that's how."

"You said anything to—to anybody about this?"

"No, not yet."

"You better not either. Mr. Darius likely would beat you half to death with his cane."

"How come that tombstone is out there, Mavis?"

Mavis suddenly pressed her lips together in a hard line, and her expression was one that told Patrick she had recovered from her surprise and was now on guard.

"It's out there in memory of Miss Cee," she said, "just like any tombstone is in memory of somebody."

"Mavis, you might as well go on and admit it, because I know. There never was a Celinda. You all just made her up because you didn't want me to know who my real mother is."

"Patrick, you're so crazy in the head that I'm scared of you. Why you want to talk crazy like that?"

"All right, if there was a Celinda, why doesn't anybody have a picture of her?"

"Somebody does. I do." Mavis put her hand over her mouth instantly as though she could call back the words and keep them from escaping again.

"Show it to me then."

"I—I can't."

"I knew it," he said disgustedly. "You tell just as many lies as the rest of them." He looked up at the picture above his head. "Jesus is looking at you, Mavis, and hearing every word you say."

Mavis sat quietly for a long time, then she got up and went to the bureau and rummaged around in the bottom drawer. When she straightened up she had a small snapshot in her hand.

She looked at the picture and her expression changed again, as though she were straining to see something from a great distance. "Mr. Darius would have a fit if he knew I had this," she said, almost under her breath. Then she gave the snapshot to him. "That was made one Easter Sunday when Miss Cee was just a little girl. See, she has on all her Easter finery."

Patrick looked at the faded snapshot. There was a little girl, about his age, standing in front of the Quincannon house. She had long blond hair and wore a big ribbon bow. Her white dress had a wide, flared skirt and a sash that must have been about a foot wide.

He looked at the picture up close, then held it out at arm's length. He looked at it from every angle, noticing every detail. Then he gave it back to Mavis. "Is that Celinda? Answer yes or no, and you'd better tell the truth, because if you don't Jesus will make something terrible happen to you."

"That's Miss Cee," Mavis said, her voice a whisper. "I can see her now just as plain. . . ."

"I can see just as plain as anything that you're still telling a story," he said. "And I thought I could trust you, Mavis. But you're just like the others."

Mavis' eyes rolled back as she looked at him. "Patrick, I declare I don't know what's wrong with you. You are plumb crazy."

He stood up. "I'm going home now, but I want you to know I'm disappointed in you, Mavis. And what's more, Jesus is disappointed, too."

She followed him to the door. "I reckon you'll get over this, Patrick—whatever it is. I keep telling myself it's growing pains and when you get your growth for the summer, you'll be just like anybody else."

"Goodbye, Mavis. I guess I'll see you at supper."

"Don't go telling Miss Athena or anybody that you were here," Mavis said. "They wouldn't like it if they knew I still have a picture of Miss Cee."

He walked back by the parking lot and counted the buses. Then when he got to the corner drugstore, he bought an ice cream cone. He didn't care if he ate ice cream until he was sick enough to die. Nobody else cared either, or they wouldn't keep lying to him all the time.

Mavis telling him that the girl in that picture was Celinda! Well, if you thought about it, maybe in a way she didn't lie too much. It *was* a picture of his mother, even if it wasn't Celinda.

Anybody who had ever seen the pictures in the Quincannon family album could have looked at Mavis' picture and known right off that the little girl with the long yellow hair and the fluffy white dress was Beryl.

Patrick let himself into the house quietly, expecting to hear Uncle Darius' gentle snores from the library and possibly the click-click of Athena's knitting needles from the living room. What he heard from the library was the sound of Uncle Darius' raised voice. Someone, probably the Yankee fellow, had dared to come during the time Uncle Darius usually had his afternoon snooze in the big chair. Patrick went to the back hall behind the stairway and listened to see if the Yankee had gone up on the offer again.

". . . But you must remember your promise," the voice said.

"I didn't promise anybody anything," Uncle Darius shouted.

"It was what she wanted. . . ."

"It was NOT what I wanted, as you well know. And now, if you don't mind. . . ."

"It's for *his* sake that I'm here," the visitor said. "He should be allowed to make the choice for himself, or at least be told that he has a choice—if that's the basis you're putting it on. Frankly, I don't think *you* have any choice in the matter."

Uncle Darius said, "I told you what was what on that score years ago, and as you can see, I haven't changed my mind. Furthermore, there isn't the remotest possibility that I ever will. Now, if you don't mind. . . ."

This time the visitor took the hint; Patrick heard a chair being pushed back, and the voice said, "Very well, Mr. Quincannon. I suppose there is nothing I can do about it at present except to continue to remember all of you in my prayers. Perhaps someday. . . ."

"You needn't be praying to your idols for me or anyone in my family," Uncle Darius said, as the two men came from the library and went to the front door. Peeping from behind the stairway, Patrick saw that the visitor was Father Conroy. He sucked in his breath in surprise, then clamped his hand over his mouth, afraid that he had been heard.

"And I don't like to be inhospitable," Uncle Darius added, "but I'd just as soon you didn't come here again."

The priest nodded and held out his hand, which Uncle Darius ignored. "Good day, Mr. Quincannon. I hope that . . ."

But Uncle Darius had closed the front door, and whatever it was that Father Conroy hoped was lost in the hot, moist breeze that blew across the front porch.

Uncle Darius went to the living room, and Patrick heard him say to Athena, "I think I handled that very well."

"Yes," Athena said. "There was nothing else you could have said, under the circumstances. I heard most of the conversation."

Patrick waited, but nothing else was said, so he went to the living room. He did not know whether he could get by with mentioning the fact that he knew Father Conroy had been there or whether, as everything seemed to have become, it was one of Uncle Darius' secrets. Uncle Darius took care of the dilemma immediately by asking, "Patrick, have you been talking to that priest?"

"You mean Father Conroy, the one who was just here?"

"That's exactly who I mean." Uncle Darius' eyes were focused on him as though they had some sort of lie-detecting device behind them, clicking away in his head.

"Did he say I had?" Patrick asked.

"Well, no, but I can't imagine why else he would have come today, out of a clear blue sky, unless you or somebody put it in his head."

Patrick didn't understand this, but he did understand that he was going to have to tell a lie in order to keep Uncle Darius from having a fit and getting purple in the face. He crossed his fingers behind him and said, "No sir, I haven't been talking to him." It was *almost* the truth, he told himself, because he and the priest hadn't actually said very much that day he went inside the church.

"I'd better not hear of your talking to him," Uncle Darius said, "or I'll . . ."

"You'll skin me alive," Patrick finished for him. "I don't hardly ever talk to *any* Catholics, Uncle Darius, except for one boy at school. And he's two grades behind me."

Athena closed the book she had been reading, holding her finger in it to keep her place. "You mustn't think Uncle Darius is prejudiced, dear," she said. "It's just that in this instance, he knows what's best for you. I mean . . ."

"In *all* instances," Uncle Darius said. "I think I'll go for a walk. That man got me so upset I'll never be able to get any rest now."

Patrick expected to hear him stop in the hall for his hat and cane and then leave by the front door, but Uncle Darius did not stop for anything, and he left by the back door. Patrick felt hot and sick as he realized where Uncle Darius was going to walk.

"Athena," he said when he had recovered enough to find his voice, "were Uncle Darius and Father Conroy talking about me?"

"Among other things," Athena said.

"Why did Father Conroy come here?"

"It was just a little soical visit," Athena said, opening her book again as though she didn't want to be disturbed, especially by questions.

"But everybody knows that Uncle Darius doesn't like Catholics or Yankees, so why would a Catholic come for a social visit?" The Yankee, he knew, had come strictly on business.

"Father Conroy does that every now and then —every year or so, I think." Athena said. "He drops in to see how we're all getting along."

"But why should he? I thought he went calling only on Catholics, the way Mr. Hancock only calls on Methodists."

"Father Conroy and Uncle Darius. . . ." Athena hesitated as though she were having a hard time explaining to him. "They knew each other a long time ago. They had some—you might call it—business dealings, and ever since then Father Conroy has been interested in the family."

"I never saw him here before," Patrick said. "And I'll bet he never comes again, because Uncle Darius told him not to." He was quiet for a time, then he asked, "What did he say about me? Father Conroy, I mean."

"Nothing much. Just asked how you were."

"Was he talking about me when he said somebody should be allowed to make a choice for himself?"

"No, dear. Now run along and play. You shouldn't spend these nice afternoons in the house."

But Patrick sat quietly on the footstool beside Athena's chair, his mind going over the fragments of conversation he had heard from the library. There was no doubt left that they had been talking about him when he came in, but what had the priest meant about a choice? *He should at least be told that he has a choice.* What kind of choice did he have that he hadn't been told about? A choice of believing or not believing about Celinda? A choice of mothers, Beryl or Athena? A choice of *what*, for crying out loud?

Obviously, the only way to find out was to go to see Father Conroy. But the priest might not tell him (he might be afraid of Uncle Darius too), and Uncle Darius would certainly lay the cane on if he ever found out Patrick was messing around the priest's house. He had already promised as much.

Patrick would have to take the chance. Tomorrow morning he would have to find Father Conroy and ask him about the choice and also ask him why he had come to see Uncle Darius, because that, to Patrick, was the strangest thing of all.

Before he had time to complete his plans in his mind, Uncle Darius was back from his walk. He came into the living room, talking excitedly even before he ascertained whether anyone was still there.

"Never saw anything like it in all my life. Athena, do you know what's happened? I just don't understand it. I was out there not more than a week ago, and everything was all right, but now. . . ."

"Out where, Uncle Darius?" Athena asked. "What are you talking about?"

Patrick could feel the color leaving his face as the blood drained down his body like sand leaving the top half of an hourglass. He knew *exactly* what Uncle Darius was talking about.

"Celinda's grave." Uncle Darius sat down across from Athena and stared at her as though he could not believe himself the startling news he had for her. "It has been ruined, absolutely ruined, by moles."

"Moles!" Athena laid her book aside this time.

"I'm sure it's moles," Uncle Darius said. "No other animal burrows underground like that and leaves ridges for tracks. Strange, too, I didn't find the tracks anywhere but over the grave. Right through the moss. And not just a track or two either. The whole grave is a mass of mole ridges."

"I never heard of such a thing," Athena gasped. "We'll have to set mole traps or we'll be besieged by them."

Weakly, Patrick sat up straighter on the footstool. The blood was going back uphill now, and his face felt as though too much blood had gone too far uphill. "I think," he said softly, "that I'll go up to my room and read for a while."

Neither Athena nor Uncle Darius heard him, and he left the room as unobtrusively as possible, thanking his lucky stars for the escape.

As he went upstairs he heard Uncle Darius saying, "I'll stop off at Crouper's Hardware in the morning and see if they have any of those mole contraptions. I cannot understand why it's only across the grave that they. . . ."

And Patrick could not understand why Uncle Darius referred to it as a grave.

Patrick was unusually quiet at supper that night, but since the others also were preoccupied, no one appeared to notice the lack of conversation—not even Uncle Darius, who thought it an "abominable display of bad manners" not to keep a conversation going at mealtime. That is, no one noticed the unusual quiet except Mavis. Patrick saw her glance inquisitively from one to the other as she served, and he was positive she was wondering if he had told about his visit to her that afternoon. She looked uncomfortable, as though her shoes were pinching her bunions. Well, she should be uncomfortable —anybody should who had tried to fool him the way she had! He decided that when she brought in the dessert, he would see what he could do to make her even more uncomfortable, really make those shoes pinch the living hell out of her.

He looked around the table again. Uncle Darius was chewing his food as though he were counting every chew, but he was also humming softly, so Patrick knew he was thinking instead of counting. His forehead had three creases which seemed to get wider every minute, like small ditches turning into ravines. Beryl had once said that the deeper Uncle Darius got into thought, the more like a newly plowed field his face became.

Beryl herself didn't look any too happy right now, but Patrick couldn't imagine what was bothering her. She had missed the afternoon visit of Father Conroy, and nobody had told her about it yet. Something must have gone wrong at the shop, but that seemed unlikely. Beryl never talked about her job, except once she had said, "It's a nothing job. It takes nothing from me, it gives me nothing. It's just a way to slaughter time, keep me occupied and off the streets." This statement had shocked Athena somewhat, and Patrick couldn't understand why, except that almost everything shocked Athena.

Beryl was feeding herself as though she were a robot. Her arm made the movements mechanically from plate to mouth, but she wasn't looking at what she was doing. She wasn't looking at anything. Her eyes stared straight ahead, across the top of Patrick's head, but the *knowing* in them had gone somewhere else. He wondered where.

Athena, on the other hand, concentrated on her

food as though it were the most important thing in the world. For some reason, she did not want to look at anybody else at the table and so she stared at the plate until, if it had been alive, it would have been hypnotized. Even when at rest, the blue eyes seemed to snap. Patrick could almost see tiny sparks flash from them, and he could almost hear the same snapping sound that his nylon hairbrush made in winter when it (or his head) was full of electricity.

Looking at the three of them, Patrick came to a conclusion that had never occurred to him before—probably, he thought, because he had lived with these people all his life and had gotten used to them. But now it came to him in the straight, unconfused manner that the thought about there being no Celinda, and either Beryl or Athena being his mother, had come.

*This whole, entire cotton-picking family is screwy as hell.*

As soon as the thought was expressed in his mind, he looked down in embarrassment, afraid that he had said the words out loud. He didn't want to hurt their feelings, and he didn't want to make them mad enough to punish him for saying "hell," to say nothing of calling them screwy. But that's exactly what they were, screwy as hell.

Making up a person who was supposed to be his mother, putting a tombstone where there was no grave, living all shut out from the world by a fence and vines (except for Beryl, who got out every day), making scrapbooks out of newspapers!

Living around a bunch of nuts like that was enough to make a person as screwy as they were.

He wondered suddenly if he *was* screwy and just hadn't realized it yet. But no, that couldn't be. He had to be sane in order to realize that they were not. He smiled to himself as he thought about how very sane he was, compared with his relatives.

And then Mavis brought the dessert, and it was time to make her uncomfortable to pay her back for lying to him.

"I made your favorite, Patrick," she said. "Chocolate pie."

He almost relented as he looked at the pie with the swirling meringue at least three inches high. But then he knew she had made the pie to bribe him into silence. Mavis should know him better than that.

"Guess what," he said, looking at Beryl, but speaking to anyone who would come out of a trance long enough to listen. "Mavis has a picture of Beryl when she was a little girl."

Mavis stopped on her way back to the kitchen and stared at him as though he had just told the family that she had a fire-breathing dragon hidden in her house. He almost laughed as he watched her face. Athena came out of her trance and said, "I'm not surprised. Mavis has lots of pictures of the family."

"Which one is it, Mavis?" Beryl asked.

"It's one of you in a white Easter dress," Patrick said. "You were about as big as me and you were standing in front of the house and you had long hair, almost down to your waist. I knew it was you right off, even if Mavis did try to fool me."

"But Beryl never had . . ." Athena began, and Beryl said suddenly, "Oh, *that* one. I thought that picture had been lost years ago. Do you still have it, Mavis?"

Mavis looked miserable. Patrick could not have hoped for better results, but he was a bit puzzled as to why Mavis should be that miserable. Maybe she was right about Uncle Darius having a fit, but why should Uncle Darius care if she had an old snapshot of Beryl?

"Yes, ma'am, I got it. I came across it in a drawer."

"Well, bring it in and let us see it sometime." Uncle Darius rejoined the world. "I don't remember any picture of Beryl in an Easter dress."

Now to make her admit that she had lied to him, and then he would let her off the hook. "It *was* a picture of Beryl, wasn't it, Mavis?"

Mavis bowed her head and did not speak for a minute.

"I said . . ." Patrick began again.

"Yes, it was Miss Beryl," Mavis said, and then fled through the pantry door and into the kitchen.

"Where did you see the picture, Patrick?" Beryl asked.

Now he was about to get in trouble, and he would have to think of a way out without lying. After all, there was enough lying going on in this house without him throwing in his nickel's worth. "Mavis showed it to me once when I was at her house." It wasn't a lie after all.

"But Beryl, I don't understand," Athena said, "You never had. . . ."

Beryl stood up suddenly. "I'll explain later," she said. "I've got to run. Natalie is coming for me in a few minutes."

"You going over there again tonight?" Uncle Darius said. "You're worse than Patrick. You're both going to wear out your welcome."

"Don't worry about it, Uncle Darius," Beryl said. "I was invited."

"May I be excused, too?" Patrick asked. He was suddenly tired of listening to his screwy relatives.

"Certainly," Uncle Darius said. "We're all finished now."

Patrick went out to the front porch and sat down in the swing for a few minutes, then he went down the walk to the iron gate. He'd sort of like to go to the Nichols' house, too, because it had been a long time since he'd seen Rusty, and he'd like to know if that fishing trip was still in the offing. He knew if he asked Athena she'd say no, it was too late for him to go now, but maybe if he waited until Beryl came out she would take his part.

He leaned back into the cool ivy on the fence and waited. Before long a car stopped in front of the gate and the horn blew. Beryl came out immediately, and just as Patrick was about to step out to the sidewalk, he realized that it was not Natalie Nichols in the car.

"I always feel like a clod, sitting out here and blowing for you," a man's voice said.

*In the tradition of* To Kill a Mockingbird, *here is a southern novel that will charm millions as it makes its author's name known throughout America.*

"It was at the beginning of the summer of his twelfth year that Patrick Quincannon Tolson reluctantly came to the conclusion that one of his aunts—either Athena or Beryl—was not his aunt at all but his mother."

This is only the first of many "conclusions" that young Patrick comes to in the course of an extraordinary summer. Deciding that he has been lied to about his supposedly dead mother, he begins—with the dedication of a superspy—to untangle the whole fabric of his life by the only means available to a boy growing up in a sheltered southern family: eavesdropping.

His search for the truth leads him to listen in secretively to the most private conversations of the people who make up his life; to hide in the back seat of the car when one aunt meets her boy friend; to search for pictures of his mother—none of which seem to exist. It also leads him to the cemetery in back of his house to dig away at the earth he has been told contains his mother's body.

Patrick's discovery, the steps leading up to it, and what he does with the truth once he finds it, make *The Sound of Summer Voices* a rare and beautiful reading experience of the kind we are allowed to have only once in a very long while. Remember the name of Patrick Quincannon Tolson, because once you

*(continued from front flap)*

eavesdrop with him, you'll forget he's a character in fiction and think of him as a memory of childhood and an unforgettable part of your own life.

Photograph by Duane Paris

HELEN TUCKER was born in Louisberg, N.C., a small town not unlike the one in *The Sound of Summer Voices*. A former newspaper reporter and writer for radio, she is now Director of Publicity and Publications at the North Carolina Museum of Art. She has been writing since she was five years old, and has published dozens of stories in national magazines.

"I try to write the kind of fiction that I, myself, like to read," she says: "With characters who make the reader forget they're reading fiction, and a story line that keeps them interested in knowing what will happen next—and caring greatly what *does* happen to the characters."

In *The Sound of Summer Voices,* her first novel, we feel that Helen Tucker has achieved exactly that.

"I know, but I told you that was the way it would have to be," Beryl said.

She got into the car, and Patrick came out of the ivy. The man Beryl was with was Christopher Danton.

Patrick wandered slowly down the sidewalk, his mind absorbed with the scene he had just witnessed. Beryl getting into the car and going off with that Yankee Danton! If Uncle Darius knew, he would throw an honest-to-God fit that would last for weeks. He would hum to himself all the time, and his nose would twitch like a rabbit's, and the Lord in His mystery only knew what else would happen. He might even skin Beryl alive.

He stopped suddenly as a new thought came to him. Danton must be Beryl's boy friend, the one Rusty had talked about. Patrick walked on slowly, and the more he thought about it, the more sense it made. Mr. Nichols was manager of the plant that Christopher Danton owned. That was how Rusty knew all about Beryl's boy friend. She had probably met him at Rusty's house in the first place. He mentally patted himself on the back as he fit the pieces nicely into the puzzle. It would be fun now to see old Rusty and just sort of casually let him know that he, Patrick, knew as much as Rusty about Beryl's boy friend.

Since he already was headed in the direction of Rusty's house, he walked faster. If he didn't stay long, he might get back home before Athena missed him. He could hardly wait to see the expression on Rusty's face. . . .

In front of the Nichols' house he stopped abruptly. Danton's car was parked in the driveway.

"What're you doing here, Patrick?" Rusty appeared on the sidewalk beside him.

"I—I just thought I'd come over to see what you're doing," Patrick said.

"Well, you can't go in the house because we've got company—secret company."

"Oh, pooh," Patrick said, his tone of voice so casual that it surprised even him. "It's only Beryl and her boy friend."

"How do you know who it is?" Rusty's expression was all that Patrick had hoped it would be.

"Because I do, that's how."

"You want to go peep at them? We can stand outside the window and see and hear them, and they won't know we're there."

"Might as well," said Patrick, still the soul of nonchalance.

They went silently to the shrubbery beneath the living room window, got on their hands and knees to crawl under the thick foliage, then stood up, flattened against the brick wall of the house.

The window was eye-level for Patrick, and it made him uncomfortable at first to have such a close view of the foursome inside. It seemed impossible to be that close to them without their knowing it.

Natalie and Louis and Beryl and Danton were in the room. Beryl and Danton sat on the sofa and the Nichols sat across the room from them. All four had glasses from which they sipped occasionally.

"They're drinking likker," Rusty whispered knowingly.

"Shh," Patrick said. He didn't want to miss anything that was being said in the room, and the shock of finding Beryl drinking spirits already had caused him to miss quite a bit. There was no question about it, if Uncle Darius could see her now he would pretty near kill her. Drinking spirits and sitting beside a Yankee who had his arm around her—well, not quite around her. His arm was resting on the back of the sofa behind her, but if she took a deep breath she'd probably touch it. Danton looked as though that was exactly what he wanted.

Beryl was laughing about something her boy friend apparently didn't think was funny. "You just have to get used to him, if you can," she said. "And you have to have a sense of humor to live with him. I don't know how Athena manages, except that sometimes I think she may be a little like him."

"A little?" Natalie echoed. "She's exactly like him, and I've never known whether it was from association or whether it was congenital."

"It isn't association," Louis said, "or Beryl would

be like him, too. How did it happen that you turned out so well?"

"She may have escaped *being* like her uncle, but she hasn't escaped *from* him," Danton said.

"She almost did once," Natalie said. "Have you ever told Chris about the car episode, Beryl?"

Beryl shook her head, and Natalie said, "Chris, you should have been here then. Beryl had a car—a sporty job it was, too, if I remember—and things were different then. Instead of having friends call for her outside the gate, she could whiz around all over the place."

"And that's where the trouble started and ended," Beryl said. "Uncle Darius made me get rid of the car."

"That's ridiculous, Beryl," Danton said. "If you bought the car yourself and you were over twenty-one, he couldn't 'make' you get rid of the car."

"Let's put it this way then," Beryl said. "It was easier to get rid of it than it was to buck Uncle Darius. And Athena was against me, too."

"That's what's wrong with Uncle Darius now," Danton said. "Nobody has ever had the guts to buck him."

"Oh, you're wrong there," Beryl said. "Even I had the guts at one time. But all the fight went out of me about ten years ago—at the time Patrick was born, when I saw how things were going to be. Oh—I was mad about the car incident, and I sulked for a while, but. . . ." She gestured helplessly and then started laughing.

"I'm glad you can find it amusing," Danton said.

"I can't. There is nothing the least bit amusing to me about Darius Quincannon."

"There are times when I couldn't agree more," Beryl said. "When I'm in that house, there are times when I think I'm losing my mind. But there are also times—like tonight—when I can talk with friends, and nothing seems very bad or very wrong in the world, and I can even laugh about Uncle Darius." She was thoughtful for a minute, then added, "And sometimes I could cry about him, too. His life hasn't been an easy one, and I try to remember that when I'm blaming him for things that aren't really his fault. You have to remember, Chris, that he was brought up with one set of values in a world that changed very little. Now he finds not only the world changing but even the set of values as well. He can't understand or accept this, and he isn't alone. I don't think there are many in his generation who can accept the so-called new morality and the de-emphasizing of the family and family ties."

"It's only in the South that Family is worshiped as a sort of secondary god," Danton said, "and Change is considered the devil."

"No, it isn't," Natalie said quickly, ready to argue. "Family ties may seem stronger in the South —I guess they are—but Southerners are no more afraid of change than any other section of the country."

"Beryl was right," Louis said. "Darius Quincannon's fear of change is not peculiar to him or his region. It's universal. No one, particularly the older ones, can bear the thought of losing everything that is familiar and valued. To lose the world you know is like a little death in itself. I can understand why he wants to hang on to the Quincannon property even though it's impractical to keep it." He stood up and reached for Danton's glass. "Who's ready?"

"No more for me, thanks," Danton said. "Beryl and I have to be going."

"And I have to call Rusty in," Natalie said. "It's time to get the heir apparent off the streets. Wait, don't go yet."

Rusty nudged Patrick in the ribs. "I've got to go before she comes out. You coming over tomorrow, Patrick?" He did not wait for an answer because the front door opened and Natalie called, "Rus-tee!"

Rusty got down on the ground and snaked his way under the shrubbery. "Yes'm, I'm coming."

"Come say goodnight to Beryl and Chris, and then skedaddle off to bed. What were you doing out there by yourself?"

"Just playing," Patrick heard him say as he went into the house.

Patrick crawled out from under the shrubbery and stood undecidedly for a minute in the yard. If he was going to escape the wrath of Athena and Uncle Darius, he'd better get a move on. But on the other hand, if he stuck around for a while longer there was no telling what all he might learn. He looked at the window again. Beryl and Danton were going to leave soon, and the Nichols might or might not say something that would interest him after their guests left. His best chance of learning something was to stick with Beryl and her boy friend. But if he got caught. . . .

He had taken enough chances lately so that one more didn't seem like much. After all, he was only trying to find out things he had a right to know.

He went to Danton's car in the driveway, opened the door, and lay down on the floor of the back seat. He had no idea where they would be going from here, but it didn't make much difference as long as they didn't find out they had a stowaway along.

A delicious sensation of fear went up his spine, and he clenched and unclenched his fists. He had never done anything like this before.

It was about twenty minutes before he heard the Nichols saying goodnight to Beryl and Danton and then saw them coming across the yard. He put his arms up around his face as though this would help him remain better hidden.

They were quiet after they got into the car. Danton backed out of the driveway, and Patrick could not tell which way he turned. They had ridden for a few minutes when Beryl said, "Well, where to tonight?"

"There's a piece of property near Briarman's Cliff I want you to see," Danton said. "This hassle with your Uncle Darius has had me looking at every piece of land in the county that might possibly be for sale."

"You're surely not thinking of putting an office building on Briarman's Cliff?" Beryl said.

"Hardly, but I want you to see this place. I'm thinking of putting something else there."

"Have you given up on our property yet? You might as well, I keep telling you. Uncle Darius is never going to sell."

"Your Uncle Darius . . . Oh, the hell with it —and him for that matter!"

"Don't take it out on me, Chris. Seems every time his name comes up, you get mad. You'll just have to learn to laugh at him, the way I do. If I couldn't laugh at him I think I'd go insane."

"I not only get mad when his name is mentioned, I can get mad just thinking about him. You and Athena both act like captive princesses who are kept hidden away in a Gothic palace. It's all right if that's what Athena wants, but my God, Beryl, you're thirty years old and—"

"Thirty-two."

"—And you have a mind of your own, and I'm damned if I can understand why you continue to live with that old bully and that cranky old maid sister."

"Athena isn't cranky, she's—"

"All right, she isn't cranky. Anything you say."

Patrick heard a movement on the front seat and he risked holding his head up just high enough to see across the back of the seat, and then he ducked down again. Beryl had moved over beside Danton and had her head on his shoulder.

"Let's not talk about it any more, please, Chris."

There was no answer and Patrick did not dare raise up again. He felt his body shift from one side to the other as the car took curves at a fairly rapid rate of speed, and he relaxed and let his body go with the movement of the car. There was no more conversation from the front seat until the car had stopped.

"Briarman's Cliff," Danton said. "And there you have your fair city at your feet."

"It's *your* fair city too, now," Beryl said. "Where is this land you wanted me to see?"

"We're parked on it," he said. "As a matter of fact, I think we're parked in our future back yard —or front yard if you'd rather the house faced this way."

Beryl said nothing.

"You do like it up here, don't you?" Danton asked.

"I love it up here, Chris. I think this would be the most beautiful spot in the world to build a house."

"*Would* be? You mean will be, don't you?"

"Will be," she corrected.

"Good. Then that's all settled. I'll talk to the architect tomorrow."

"Not tomorrow, Chris. Not yet."

There was a long, exasperated sigh. "Yes, it will be tomorrow, Beryl. We're not going to wait any longer for you to try to think up some way to break the news to your uncle. I'm losing my patience fast. If you were sixteen it would be different . . ."

"Please, Chris, let's not go through that again. You don't understand and there's no way I can make you understand. I know I am going to have to break with Uncle Darius—and maybe Athena too—but I can't—not just yet. Please trust my judgment in this."

Danton tried a new tack. "Sometimes I think you're as eccentric as your uncle, but I love you anyway."

"Prove it." Patrick could tell from her voice that Beryl had that saucy, teasing look on her face, the one she sometimes had when she was making fun of Uncle Darius and winking at Patrick.

"That's easy enough. Will you come with me into the house?" Danton got out of the car and Beryl followed him, sliding under the steering wheel on his side. Patrick raised up to see where they were going and saw they hadn't gone anywhere. They were standing beside the car, locked together, only their heads moving. They seemed to be trying to devour each other as hungrily as though neither of them had had a square meal for six months. Patrick almost uttered Mavis' favorite exclamation, "Jesus God!" but caught himself just in time.

"We are standing on the terrace," Danton finally said. "If you'll come with me through the French doors, I'll show you the way to the bedroom."

Patrick watched them walking hand in hand across the clearing to the other side of the cliff, and then they were just two dark shadows and he could no longer hear what they were saying. He saw Danton take off his jacket and spread it on the ground, and he saw Beryl sit down on the jacket and hold up her arms to Danton. At that point Patrick sneezed. The warm, heavily sweet odor of honeysuckle from the side of the cliff was getting to him and getting to him good. He sneezed again and quickly lay down on the floor of the car, holding his finger tightly across his upper lip. If they found him now he'd be skinned alive even before Uncle Darius got a chance at him.

It was a long, long time before Beryl and Danton came back to the car, and Patrick was almost asleep when he heard the door open. He started violently and sat up, then quickly hit the floor again, hoping he had not been discovered.

Danton started the car and turned it around, and they were coasting down the hill and taking the curves. Neither of them spoke until they were back inside the city limits, and then Danton said, "How much longer are you going to make it necessary for us to go on this way?"

"Not much longer, I promise you, Chris. There's just one thing that has to be worked out. . . ." She stopped suddenly, and Patrick heard that soft laugh of hers, like the tinkle of thin crystal. "I would never have believed it, but I think this bothers you more than it does me. Sometimes I believe you are actually shocked."

"Mark it up to my middle-class morality," Danton said.

Beryl's soft laugh came again, but she did not answer. Patrick wanted to sit up and see what was going on, but he didn't dare. And besides, he had just had a thought that made him break out in a cold sweat. Danton was undoubtedly taking Beryl home now, and he would put her out at the gate and then drive off—with Patrick in the back seat. What in tarnation was he going to do to get out of this mess?

The car stopped, and Patrick knew they were in front of the iron gate because he could smell the evergreens. His nose started twitching again, and both hands went up to stop the sneeze. He succeeded, and waited for Beryl to get out of the car, but nobody seemed to be making a move to get out. He started to peep over the seat but decided not to. They were probably kissing again. That was about all they'd done since they left the Nichols' house. They had acted like a couple of goofs up on Briarman's Cliff, pretending they were in a house and smooching like movie stars—at least he supposed that was what they were doing while he was half asleep in the car, practically knocked out with boredom. One thing for sure, it had been a wasted evening as far as he was concerned. He had thought they would say something that would answer some of his questions, but all he'd learned was that Beryl was probably going to marry Danton, thus causing Uncle Darius to have a fit.

"I have to go in now," Beryl said. "Tomorrow night?"

"No, I have to go out of town for a few days. I'll call you at the shop when I get back."

There was another long silence, and then Patrick heard the door open. He raised up and saw that it was the door on Danton's side and that Danton was getting out. Beryl slid out after him and they went to the gate.

Patrick took a deep breath. This probably would be his best and only chance to get out of the car. As quietly as possible, he opened the door on the street side and slipped out. He pushed the door to, but did not close it completely for fear of being heard. Now that he was in the street, there was nothing to do but stoop beside the car and hope that by the time Danton drove off, Beryl would have gone through the gate. He also hoped that no cars would pass in the meantime and shine their lights on him.

It took Beryl and Danton an awful long time to say goodnight at the gate, but finally Patrick heard him get in the car, and then the car moved slowly away from the curb. He closed his eyes tightly, afraid to look toward the gate, and waited to see if he would hear an exclamation from Beryl. When none came, he opened his eyes and went to the sidewalk. Beryl was beyond the gate, going up the walk to the house. He waited until she went inside and then followed, knowing that now he faced the worst ordeal of all.

The front door would be locked. Beryl had a key, but of course he didn't. He would either have to run and catch up and go in with her, or ring the bell and raise Athena and Uncle Darius, or sleep on the porch all night.

And then, as he debated the first two choices in his mind, Beryl slipped inside the house.

Immediately Patrick cursed himself for being a dumb-stupid cretin. As soon as Beryl was inside, it seemed that every light in the house went on at once, and he could hear voices raised like in the next-to-the-last scene of a monster movie when the monster is being captured.

"Beryl, thank-God-you're-back-have-you-seen-Patrick-where-have-you-been-I-called-Natalie-and-she-said-you-weren't-there-that-you-had-left." All this from Athena, spouting off about a mile a minute like the drinking fountain on the courthouse square when someone tried to see how high the water would go.

"Where *is* he, Beryl? That boy will be the death of us yet. We thought he had gone to Rusty's until Athena called Natalie."

"No," Beryl said. "I haven't seen Patrick. He wasn't with Rusty." Then there was alarm in her voice. "My God, it's two A.M. Where could he be?"

"Something terrible has happened this time," Athena said. "I just know it. We were sure—at least we were hoping—that he was with you. I thought about calling Natalie back to find out, but it was so late I hated to bother her and . . . Oh Lord in heaven, what are we going to do?"

"This time we're going to call the police," Beryl said, then added, "You *have* looked in his room, haven't you?"

"We've searched every inch of this house and grounds," Uncle Darius said. "The boy has simply disappeared. We haven't seen him since supper."

Patrick was going to have to lie again. He pressed a fist into the top of his head to make himself think faster, then opened the front door and went into the hall. The lights blinded him, and he rubbed his eyes.

"Patrick!" Athena was practically screaming. "Patrick, are-you-all-right-where-have-you-been-my-Lord-we've-been-looking-for-you-for-hours."

"Yes, ma'am, I'm all right." He stopped rubbing his eyes, blinked, and said: "I was under the front porch, asleep in my cave. Beryl woke me up when she came in walking on top of me."

*"Under the porch asleep!"* Uncle Darius had his mental lie detector clicking away, and it did not seem to be working in Patrick's favor. "That is the most absurd statement I have ever heard from you, Patrick. Why would you go to sleep under the porch? We called and called you, and had you been on the premises, you would have heard us."

"Not if I was asleep," he said, determined to stick to the story.

"We called loud enough to arouse the dead," Uncle Darius said. "Athena will bear me out."

Athena bore him out.

Patrick looked from one to the other and then to Beryl. "When she walked across the porch it woke me up." He knew as soon as he said it that it was the wrong thing. Beryl had been tiptoeing, because the last thing in the whole, entire world she wanted was to wake up Uncle Darius at two A.M. Beryl gave him a funny look and said, "Well, as long as he's all right, I'm going to bed. I'll see you in the morning." She went upstairs in a hurry, and Patrick knew she was getting out of the way before Uncle Darius started asking her questions about where she had been for so long and why she wasn't at Natalie's when Athena called.

"Where have you been, Patrick?" The way Athena looked at him reminded him of a picture in his history book of a stormtrooper at an inquisition.

"Under the porch asleep." He closed his eyes, waiting for the various methods of torture to begin —the bucket of water dripping slowly on his head, the burning matches applied to his flesh, the rack which would stretch him until he was big as a sixteen-year-old.

"Patrick, you will go to your room now." Uncle Darius' voice was a monotone, and each word, each syllable, was pronounced precisely, as though it were the last word that would ever be heard while the world stood. "You will go to your room, and you will remain there all day tomorrow, all the next day, and the day after that. You will, in fact, not be permitted to leave these premises until you can tell us the truth about where you have been tonight. We will put up with these disappearing acts of yours no longer. Neither will we put up with a liar. Remember, Patrick, the Lord abhors a lying tongue."

Patrick muttered a few words about not having always been told the truth in this household himself, and then, on catching sight of Uncle Darius' expression, closed his mouth.

"What was that?" Uncle Darius looked as though he was ready to take his cane out of the umbrella stand by the door and let Patrick have it.

"I said . . . Nothing." He started up the stairs, and when he reached the top step he looked down at the two upturned faces that had watched every step of his progress. "I was so too asleep under the porch. So there!" He went to his room and slammed the door. Then he waited, shaking almost visibly, for Athena to come up and spank him for slamming the door. But no one came, and a few minutes later he heard Uncle Darius and Athena come upstairs and go to their rooms.

He realized now for the first time that he was

very sleepy, so sleepy that he didn't think he'd mind staying in his room for three days and sleeping all that time. But just before he closed his eyes a thought occurred to him. Tomorrow was the day he had planned to go to see Father Conroy and find out what the priest meant about his having a choice of some kind.

# 10

Patrick got through the first day of his imprisonment painlessly and with little or no boredom. He slept a great deal, read a great deal, and was quite cheerful when Mavis brought his meals to him on a tray. The second day, which was Sunday, started out even better than the first when he realized that he would not have to go to Sunday School. He could stay in his room and read about mysteries and their solutions, while the other kids would have to get all gussied up and go hear about the Divine Mystery which had no explanation that he could ever understand.

The morning passed quickly, and Mavis brought his tray. Fried chicken, mashed potatoes with gravy, string beans, and strawberry shortcake. He had been surprised at the food, for he had expected Uncle Darius to see that he got only prison fare—probably a glass of water and cold grits. He was also surprised that none of the family had come in to see him. He had never been banished to his room for so long a time before, and he had thought Beryl or Athena, at least, might have looked in to be sure he wasn't sick or anything. This began to weigh on his mind after he finished the chicken.

They were all the time carrying on about how he didn't look well or how he was acting strangely or something, and here he was under the same roof and could be dying of beri-beri or scurvy or sleeping sickness or some other thing like that, and they didn't even poke their heads in the door to ask how he felt. It would serve them right if his soul slipped quietly into heaven without their knowing anything about it, and if when they came to tell him he could leave the room they found his lifeless body on the bed, his eyes staring at them coldly and accusingly in death.

He amused himself with this thought for a long time. He could picture Athena weeping beside the bed, saying, "May the Lord forgive us for what we have done to this dear boy. Oh Patrick, Patrick, come back to us." And Uncle Darius would be too broken up to talk. He would just stand there in the doorway, his nose twitching, his face turning purple in agony. And Beryl. . . .

Here he paused in his fantasy, for he could not imagine how Beryl would react to his death. A few days ago he could have predicted, but now he did not know Beryl as well as he used to, and the more he thought about her, the less he knew her. Would she cry and say to Uncle Darius, "My sweet little boy! What have you done to him?" and then cling to Athena, or would she look at him and show no emotion to the others and then go out and find Christopher Danton and cry with her head on his shoulder?

One thing for sure, Uncle Darius probably would see to it that he was buried beside Celinda's tombstone in the back yard. Would they put up a new tombstone for him, or would the one which was already there and marked no grave be enough?

As he tried to imagine what his funeral in the woods would be like, he decided that he definitely did not want to be buried out there by himself. Maybe if there really were a Celinda buried there it would be different, but to be put out there all alone. . . .

These thoughts weren't quite so entertaining as the ones about the family's first reaction to his passing, so he picked up his book again and continued reading the adventures of a twelve-year-old detective who put the hometown police force to shame.

Since Mavis was off on Sunday nights, Uncle Darius brought the evening tray. He placed it on the table beside the bed and turned to Patrick, who was sitting on the window seat looking out toward the woods.

"Well, my boy, I trust by now you have had enough of solitary confinement and are ready to amend your ways."

Patrick stared at him without answering.

"Are you ready to make a full confession of your activities on Friday night?"

There was a long silence and then Patrick said,

"I don't have anything to confess." Uncle Darius clearly had had no pangs of conscience about leaving his great-nephew alone in the hardships and pain of beri-beri, scurvy, and sleeping sickness. That Patrick might die forlorn and forgotten in his room apparently had not been part of Uncle Darius' afternoon musings.

"Where were you Friday night, Patrick, while Athena and I searched for you?"

"I was under the porch asleep." Maybe if Uncle Darius' tone of voice had been more relenting, Patrick would have felt worse about the lie.

"I see you are not yet ready to leave your room and take up your rightful place in a truth-loving, respectable family," Uncle Darius said.

"No, sir. I guess not."

"Patrick, it is so easy to tell the truth and so hard to tell a lie." Uncle Darius sat down on the side of the bed. "Have you stopped to consider how much deception is involved in one little lie? You have to go on lying, each lie bigger than the last, to get out of the original one. And even then you never get out of it. Oh, what a tangled web we weave . . ."

"When first we practice to deceive." Patrick had heard him say that about a million times.

"You know the words," Uncle Darius nodded, "but I see they have no meaning for you." He paused, then said, "Patrick, if you'd like to tell me where you were, I will forgive you for lying to us the other night, and you may leave your room in the morning. Otherwise, you will stay here all day tomorrow and then be restricted to the grounds for the rest of the week."

Patrick was thoughtful. He *was* getting mighty tired of the old room, and by tomorrow he knew he would be going as stir-crazy as those convicts he had seen in a movie once. But to tell would mean telling on Beryl and uncovering things that would set Uncle Darius in an all-time rage. Besides, he thought nobly, he wasn't about to accept a bribe from Uncle Darius any more than he would from Mavis, who had thought chocolate pie would buy him off. He remained quiet.

"Where did you go Friday night, Patrick?"

"I was asleep under the porch."

"I see you do not realize the seriousness of what you are doing and saying." Uncle Darius stood up and went to the door. "Remember this, Patrick, if you never remember anything I've ever said to you: no liar shall enter therein."

With that Uncle Darius left and Patrick set himself about the task of eating the sandwiches Athena had sent up.

In a way he wanted to talk to Beryl, but he knew that would never do, because he could not let her know that he had been with her when she was with her boy friend. At least, he couldn't let her know yet. Maybe later it would be to his advantage to make some kind of deal with her. Tell her he would keep certain things to himself if she would reveal certain things to him. Like why they had dreamed up a Celinda to fool him.

He took the tray and put it outside his door and then went back to the window seat and watched the sunset. Out there the tombstone would be turning pink now—out there where Celinda, beloved daughter of Donald and Sarah Quincannon, was supposed to be, and wasn't.

No matter how hard he tried, he still could not think of Celinda and Beryl as one person. There *had* to have been a Celinda, because he had loved her so much. How could you love someone so much if they never existed? Surely, if by no other way, she had existed because of his love. But by the same token, she had died of his curiosity. He wished now that he had never dug up the grave, that he had never found out for sure that there was no Celinda. He could fill in his own dates on the tombstone now. Celinda was born with the first story he had heard about her, when he had first begun to worship the blonde angel of Mavis' description, and she had died last week with the dream he had carried all his whole life.

Could he ever cherish Beryl in the way that he had cherished the dream of Celinda? Maybe. But Beryl was so real, and. . . .

Tears ran down his cheeks. He did not know why he was crying; it was a dumb-stupid thing to do. Ten-year-olds didn't go around acting like babies. He bit his lip, but the tears kept coming. Everything was so confused. Beryl and Celinda, the lies the truth-loving Uncle Darius had told him, Athena's stolid respectability and propriety.

He was sobbing now, and he beat his fists against the window seat. "Who am I, anyway?" he said over and over again, unaware that he was talking out loud. "I want to know who I am." And then,

"Why isn't there a Celinda? Don't go away, Celinda. Don't leave me." It appeared that the crying spell had set in in earnest.

On Tuesday morning Athena stuck her head in the door and said, "Patrick, you may join us for breakfast. You can also go outside the house today, but you are not, under any circumstances, to set foot off the grounds. Do you hear?"

Patrick nodded.

"Uncle Darius is being very lenient with you, all things considered," Athena went on. "He is not going to mention your misconduct to you again— unless you wish to talk about it, that is, in which case he'll listen to any reasonable explanation you may have. On the other hand, you are not to be misled into believing that he has forgotten what you have done just because he doesn't bring up the subject. Any further irregularities in your behavior will go very hard with you indeed. Do you understand?"

He nodded again.

"After breakfast you are to resume helping him with his paste-ups. Come downstairs now. We are ready to eat."

He went into the dining room and looked from one to the other, and the way they looked at him would have made him feel guilty even if his past behavior had been like that of a young Jesus Christ. The expression on Uncle Darius' face almost made him want to declare loudly and passionately, "I was asleep under the porch all the time."

But he took his seat without a word.

"Good morning, Patrick," Uncle Darius said.

"Good morning." He stared at the tablecloth.

"It's good to have you back with us, Patrick," Beryl said.

He looked across at her, suddenly as glad to see her as if he—or she—had been away for months. She was once again his ally, and he would never, never tell about Friday night. Maybe he would never even tell her. He expected her to be smiling at him, the way she did when she was teasing Uncle Darius. But her expression was quite solemn, almost as though she had been one of the instigators of his punishment. It was possible that Athena and Uncle Darius had given her a rough time over the weekend, too, asking questions about why she was out so late. But Beryl could cope with that sort of thing much better than he could, because she had had more years of practice.

"Thank you," he said, and winked at her, but she did not wink back. Disappointed and hurt, he stared again at the tablecloth.

Breakfast was a quiet affair, and he was glad when it was over. He felt that in some way his presence had caused them to be struck dumb, or maybe they didn't feel like talking with a liar in their midst. It didn't matter, he supposed, that they had lied to him all his life.

He followed Uncle Darius into the library and sat down at the desk, ready to begin pasting the clippings in the scrapbook. And from the dining room where Athena was helping Mavis clear the table, he heard Athena say, "I declare he gets more like Jaybird Tolson every day. I guess we've been too lax in the discipline department, but from now on. . . ."

He did not hear what was in store for him from now on, because Uncle Darius was talking. "We'll finish this book today, and then I'll go downtown and buy a new one before tomorrow."

"Yes, sir."

For a while there was no sound in the room except that of Uncle Darius' scissors cutting the newspaper. Athena and Mavis were in the kitchen, and from the library it was not possible to hear their conversation.

Patrick took the clippings as they were given to him, put paste on the corners, and stuck them in the book. Occasionally he read the headlines of the stories, but not often. He wasn't much interested in what went on another world away when his own world had become so complex.

"Don't you ever put anything in the book that happens in the United States?" he asked.

"Of course I do," Uncle Darius said. "Patrick, I told you when you began helping me that I wanted you to observe the kind of thing I use so that when you take over you'll know just what is news and what isn't. Now, you study these clippings when I give them to you."

"All right." He looked carefully at the next one, which was about the United States. It was about Congress not cooperating with the President, or something like that.

"Do you ever put stuff that happens right here in Laurelton in the scrapbook?" he asked.

"Not very often," Uncle Darius said. "Only in

rare cases where it is an item of unusual interest, or when something happens in Laurelton that I think is of historical importance, and that is rarer still."

Athena appeared at the library door. "Uncle Darius, Louis Nichols is on the phone and . . ."

"Tell Louis if he's going to start that foolishness again about our property, he can go to the devil. I don't want to hear another word about it."

"No, this is something else," Athena said. "He said he's taking Rusty fishing up at the lake this afternoon and they want Patrick to go, too. He said they'd stay overnight and come back tomorrow morning."

"Yes!" Patrick cried. "Tell him I'll be ready." He jumped up from the desk to start getting his fishing gear together.

"One moment, Patrick." Uncle Darius ran his hand through his sparse white hair and there seemed to be just a tinge of purple added to his complexion. "You realize, of course, that you cannot leave the premises for the rest of this week."

"But this is different," Patrick said. "Mr. Nichols promised to take us last week and . . ." He broke off, realizing that it was utterly useless to try to explain anything to Uncle Darius. But he absolutely *had* to go on that fishing trip, because Mr. Nichols had promised it, and he had been looking forward to it for a long time, and it wasn't fair of Uncle Darius to ruin *every*thing.

"There is one way you can go, Patrick," Uncle Darius said. Athena stood silently in the doorway, waiting to see what word to take back to Louis. Her eyes never left Patrick's face.

Patrick waited to hear the one way he could go, afraid he already knew what it would be.

"You may go on the trip with Louis and Rusty if you will, right here and now, tell us where you were Friday night and apologize for lying and for the anxiety you caused us."

Patrick put his hands in his pockets and clenched his fists. "Why don't you believe me when I tell you something? You don't believe anything I say. I told you . . ."

"Don't start that again," Uncle Darius said. "If you want to go, I'm ready to listen to the truth. Apparently you don't want to go badly enough, though. Athena, tell Louis . . ."

"Wait a minute," Patrick said. He stared down at the pattern in the rug, tracing a large flower petal with the toe of his shoe. If he told them and apologized, he could go, no matter how mad Uncle Darius became, because Uncle Darius never broke a promise, and maybe by the time he got back tomorrow Uncle Darius would have simmered down some. All he had to say was, "I went to Rusty's and then followed Beryl." After that, it would be up to Beryl to do the explaining—except that he knew Uncle Darius would never let him stop there. He would have to tell it all.

So all right. He'd tell it all. In the long run Uncle Darius would be madder at Beryl than at him. He might get off with just a little lecture, but Beryl. . . .

What would it do to Beryl if he told? It would mean she couldn't see Christopher Danton any more. Uncle Darius would see to that. He might even make her stay in her room for a month, and if three days was a long time, think what a month would be. He knew suddenly exactly what it would be like if he told. It would be like the time Uncle Darius made Beryl get rid of the car. She would be unhappy for a long, long time and maybe not speak to any of them or maybe. . . . The new thought caused a real pain in the pit of his stomach. Maybe she would run away from home, go off with Danton the way she had once gone off with Jaybird Tolson, and then she would come back and have another baby and shame the family all over again, and then Uncle Darius would start telling even bigger lies and the new baby would grow up just the way he, Patrick, had, wondering all the time who he was.

He looked Uncle Darius straight in the eye and said, "I was asleep under the porch, and if you don't believe it I don't care."

"Athena, tell Louis Patrick appreciates the invitation but he is being punished for misbehavior and will not be able to go this time."

Athena left the room, and Uncle Darius said, "Now we'll go on with our work."

But Patrick suddenly could not stand the sight of the room, the scrapbook, or Uncle Darius for another minute. He bolted from the room, ran down the hall, and almost bumped into Mavis as he went through the kitchen. He heard Uncle Darius call, "Patrick, come back here," but he paid no attention. He was out the back door and running through the woods before Uncle Darius could get to the door to call him again.

He ran and ran and did not stop until he reached the tombstone. Then he sat down and leaned against the stone, his sides hurting from running so fast. As he struggled to get his breath, his eyes fell upon the grave, and in spite of the gasps that were all but choking him, he laughed out loud. The ridges in the moss where he had tried to fit the clumps back together really *did* look like mole paths. It was a good thing Uncle Darius had thought of that all by himself, because Patrick never in all his life could have come up with a lie good enough to cover the truth about Celinda's torn-up grave. He laughed and laughed, until he felt the tears running down his cheeks and realized that he had also been digging his heels into the moss, tearing up even more the grave that was not a grave.

# 11

He stayed in the woods most of the morning, and when he returned to the house Athena was on the back porch as though she had been standing there ever since he left, waiting for him.

"Uncle Darius wants to see you in the library immediately, Patrick," she said.

Patrick didn't answer, but he marched to the library, perfectly sure now how all those French people felt when they went to get their heads chopped off. But Uncle Darius did not say a word about the way he had run out of the house. All he said was, "If you are ready now, Patrick, we will finish our morning's work before lunch."

Patrick sat down at the desk in front of the open scrapbook, working silently and quickly to paste in the clippings Uncle Darius had laid beside the book. Uncle Darius stood over his left shoulder and watched him. The only sounds in the room were the ticking of the grandfather clock in the corner and Uncle Darius' somewhat irregular breathing, which Patrick found annoying because it was not in tempo with the clock.

When he had pasted in the last clipping, Uncle Darius bent over him and took the book. "I'll mark the inclusive dates on the outside, and then you can take the book to the attic and file it with the others. Tomorrow we'll begin a new one."

Uncle Darius dipped his pen into the inkwell and wrote on the front of the book, then blew it dry and gave it to Patrick. "See that it is on top of the book dated right before this one."

"Yes, sir." He went to the back hall where the stairway to the attic was, opened the door, and looked at the stairs for several minutes before he could find the nerve to go up. He didn't go to the attic very often, because it was a dark, gloomy place, even with the light on, and once Beryl had remarked that she expected to see bats flying around every time she went up. This was enough to keep Patrick out, since he was afraid of all kinds of bats except the vampire bats he saw in horror movies, and he figured he might be afraid of them, too, if he ever saw one in person.

He held to the railing as he went up the steps. On the far side of the suffocatingly stuffy room were the forty-seven scrapbooks stacked on the floor against the wall. Patrick checked the dates of the books in the last stack and added the forty-eighth to the heap. It was, to his way of thinking, one big mess of a way to spend your time, and he knew perfectly well that left to his own devices he would never keep up Uncle Darius' work. He looked at the dates on the books in the stack next to the current one. Each book, apparently, covered a period of about six months, and as he thumbed through one of them, the futility of what Uncle Darius was doing struck him even more. The clippings were turning quite yellow, even some of the fairly recent ones, and in a few years it would be next to impossible to read them. He wondered if Uncle Darius knew this. Maybe he should take a look at the older ones.

He went to the first few stacks and looked at the top books. The clippings in these not only were yellow and brittle, but there were dark brown splotches where the paste had been. If Uncle Darius thought anybody was ever going to pay any money for these scrapbooks, he was just plain out of his head. He'd be willing to bet you couldn't *give* the books away, even to the museum keeper, and maybe not even to the junk man.

He looked through the next stack and the next, occasionally scanning some of the clippings to see if Uncle Darius had always used dull stuff about wars in far-off countries and Presidents not getting along with Congress, and decided that he had and that the books couldn't possibly be any duller. Except for an occasional picture, they were duller than his history books, and of course the print was much harder to read. Most of the pictures were of people who were just staring straight into the camera, or of two or three people sitting at a table or something. There was a picture of Eisenhower playing golf on the White House lawn, and there was a picture of Queen Elizabeth riding sidesaddle with a long dress on, and the horse had his head turned as though he were looking at the Queen instead of where he was going. He turned a few more pages in the book dated Jan. 1, 1960, to June 30, 1960, and was about to put the book down when one picture near the back caught his eye. It showed wreckage from an airplane crash strewn around a field with only the tail section, which stuck up out of the ground as though it had been planted, recognizable. There were two men in the picture poking through the wreckage.

Patrick looked at the clipping beneath the picture, wondering why Uncle Darius had put a plane crash in his book. It was hardly a historical event, and it hadn't even happened anywhere near Laurelton. The headline said: Thirty-four Dead and Three Critically Injured in Indiana Plane Crash. He read the story and still could find no reason for its inclusion in the scrapbook. An airliner going from New York to San Francisco had crashed in Indiana. Only three of the thirty-seven people aboard had survived the crash, and they were listed as critical in a Fort Wayne hospital.

He was about to close the book when a name

suddenly jumped up at him as though the print were raised. The thirty-four dead people were listed beneath the three survivors, and one of the survivors was Jason Tolson.

Patrick looked at the name for several seconds, his heart pounding, as he established the connection in his conscious mind between the name in type and himself. The name he had been taught it was almost a sin to say was right here in Uncle Darius' book. His father had survived a plane crash in Indiana when he, Patrick, was only two years old. He immediately resented the fact that this vital piece of information had been withheld from him. Regardless of what they all thought of Jason—even Beryl, who must have loved him at one time—it wasn't fair not to tell his son something exciting about him, like how he was in a plane crash and all. It made Jason sort of a hero because he had survived.

He looked at the picture of the wreckage for a long time, and then closed the book and replaced it on the stack. Of course it wouldn't do any good to ask any of them anything about Jason. They'd probably make up something like the Celinda lies and think he was dumb-stupid enough to believe them. But he was going to find out about Jason Tolson if it was the last thing he ever did. He had never given too much thought to Jason—mostly he had thought about Celinda, and how she had to come back home, and Jason had not come with her, and although not fully aware of it, he had resented his father. His questions about Jaybird had therefore been few. But now he wanted to know desperately.

Now he was faced with the actual *existence* of a father who before had been even more in the shadows than the mythical Celinda.

Tonight he was going to find out all he wanted to know about Jason Tolson, and he knew exactly how to go about it. Maybe—who knew?—he might even end up visiting his father somewhere, or maybe if he wrote to Jaybird he would come and take Patrick away. Maybe he would take Beryl away, too, if she wanted to go. Of course, she would have to admit to Patrick then that there never had been a Celinda and that she, Beryl, was his real mother. Perhaps she'd rather stay in Laurelton and marry Christopher Danton than go away with her old boy friend.

Regardless of what was what, and who wanted to do what, he aimed to find out everything tonight. In spite of his earlier decision that he would never tell on Beryl—and maybe he wouldn't have to if she cooperated—there were times when a little simple blackmail was necessary.

Patrick managed to get through the rest of the day somehow, although time dragged for him. He spent most of the afternoon in the swing on the front porch weighing different plans to get Beryl alone when she got home from work. Of course Uncle Darius would walk home with her, and they would join Athena in the living room until supper. There appeared to be no way he could see her alone until bedtime, and if she went out to meet Danton tonight, there was no telling how late bedtime would be.

He lived through supper, which was not as quiet as breakfast and lunch had been. Although no remarks were addressed directly to him, the others kept a semblance of conversation going among themselves. After supper he waited with something more than passing interest to find out if Beryl was meeting Danton. When she said nothing about going out, he asked finally, "Are you going over to Rusty's tonight, Beryl?"

"No, why?"

"I was just going to tell you to tell Rusty to come to see me tomorrow, is all."

Uncle Darius lowered the newspaper and peered over the top of his reading glasses. "Perhaps I forgot to mention, Patrick, that you are not to receive company this week, nor make telephone calls, nor receive telephone calls."

"I only wanted to know if they caught many fish."

"You can find out next week." The newspaper again became a screen between them.

"Want to play a game of canasta or something, Beryl?"

"No thanks, dear. Not tonight. I'm going to wash my hair and do my nails."

The TV set was blank and silent, and he almost made a move to turn it on, then decided that TV was probably out, too, along with visits and phone calls.

"I think I'll go to my room and read," he said.

"Good night, Patrick," Athena said, and Beryl smiled at him apologetically as though she were really sorry she couldn't play cards with him, and

Uncle Darius mumbled something from behind the newspaper.

He went to his room and put on his pajamas, then he went to Beryl's room to wait for her to come upstairs to wash her hair. He could talk to her then.

Beryl's room looked exactly like Beryl. It was a bright, cheerful room, filled with soft colors, pale yellows and grays, and there were frills here and there (a ruffle around the bedspread and the skirt of the vanity table), so that the room could never be mistaken for Athena's. Athena's room was filled with heavy mahogany furniture, and the predominant color was a dark, uninteresting brown.

He had brought his book, so he got into Beryl's bed, turned on the bed light and read for a long time, engrossed in the adventures of the first kids to reach the moon—Ralph and Rhonda, eleven-year-old twins whose father was an astronaut and took them along for the ride. They, of course, got lost and weren't around when the rocket took off for earth again. So there they were, stranded on the moon, wondering if there were any moon creatures around and if the creatures would come to their rescue or eat them alive.

He read for a long time, but Beryl did not come. He could not imagine what was keeping her, because she always washed her hair in the bathroom they shared. She had a little hose thing that she hooked to the faucet and turned on her head.

He closed his eyes for a minute to rest them, and when he opened them again Beryl was standing beside the bed and smiling at him. "Who's been sleeping in my bed?"

He sat up and blinked several times. It must be very late, because he could no longer hear the mumble of voices downstairs. That meant that Athena and Uncle Darius had already gone to bed.

"I came to talk to you, Beryl," he said.

"Oh? I thought you had come to evict me from my bed."

"I want you to tell me all about Jason Tolson."

Beryl's mouth dropped slightly, but she recovered quickly and gave no other sign of surprise. "Patrick, why have you suddenly started asking all these questions? You've already been told about as much as any of us know about him."

"I'm tired of being lied to, Beryl," he said matter-of-factly. "I think it's time to put a stop to this lying business right now."

"Who has lied to you, Patrick?"

"Who hasn't?"

Beryl sat down on the side of the bed, staring at him silently.

"What happened to my father after the plane crash? Why hasn't he ever been to see me?"

This time Beryl did not conceal her surprise. "How did you know about the plane crash?"

"I read about it in one of Uncle Darius' scrapbooks."

"Oh, I see. I didn't know Uncle Darius put that sort of thing in his books."

"You'd better tell me what I want to know, Beryl, or I'll . . ."

"You'll what, Patrick?"

"I'll tell that you and. . . ." He stopped, unable to go on. Beryl looked so nice, so nice and kind and sort of like a little girl with her hair hanging down that way, that he could not go on with his threat. He simply could not bring himself to tattle on Beryl, or even to threaten her with telling.

"You'll tell what, Patrick?" She had picked up a hairbrush, and now she brushed her hair absently as she looked at him.

"About my father. Nobody else will tell, and I've *got to know*."

There was a long silence.

"Yes, I suppose you do. Poor little boy." She ran her hand through his hair, messing it up, then she got up and went to the window, still brushing her own hair occasionally. After a long time she turned and looked at him.

"You will know the whole story one of these days, Patrick," she said slowly. "I think you're old enough to know most of it. Certainly if you're old enough to have curiosity about it, you're old enough to get a few of the answers. But Uncle Darius doesn't want to discuss any of it, ever. Eventually he's going to have to tell you part of it, anyway, and you'll probably hear the rest from other people. I was in favor of telling you the truth from the beginning—letting you grow up with it so it wouldn't seem strange to you. But Uncle Darius said no, and—I don't know—maybe he's right. Anyway, both Athena and I gave our word when you were just a baby that we would never say certain things in your presence. So there is nothing I can say now, Patrick."

He knew now what the height of frustration was—to be so close to all the answers and then have them withheld.

"Why can't you tell me what happened to him after the plane crash? What's so wrong about being in a plane crash? He couldn't help that."

"Nothing, Patrick. It's just that I can't talk to you about any of it, as much as I'd like to." She sat down beside him again. "However, since you found out that much from Uncle Darius' paste-ups, it might be that you could find out more the same way. And that way, I wouldn't be breaking a promise."

He got out of bed quickly and started for the door.

"Not tonight," Beryl said. "It's too late. Wait until morning. Athena and Uncle Darius might hear you in the attic."

"I'll be quiet," he said. "I want to know right this minute." He went out and closed the door, then reopened it and whispered. "Good night, Beryl," and went out again.

He went to his room and got his flashlight, because he did not dare turn on the light in the hall. The stairs to the attic looked spookier than ever, and if the bats were ever going to swarm, they couldn't pick a better time than right now. Only his gnawing need to know kept him from turning back and waiting until morning.

He stepped across the china doll that looked

like Beryl, and in the beam of the flashlight the doll looked like a dead baby sprawled across the floor. He moved her aside with his foot and found the scrapbook in which he had seen the clipping about the plane crash. He read the story again, although he already knew everything it said. Then he began to look for more clippings about his father. He did not have to look far. Two pages over there was a second, and presumably last, story.

## EX-HUSBAND OF HEIRESS
## DIES FOLLOWING CRASH

Fort Wayne, Ind.—Jason Tolson, ex-husband of furniture heiress Bonita Devond, and one of three survivors from Sunday's airplane crash here, died this morning at a local hospital from complications resulting from internal injuries received in the crash which killed thirty-four persons. Two other survivors are still listed as critical at the hospital.

Tolson was the fourth husband of Miss Devond, having married her in Las Vegas, Nev., a year ago after she obtained a divorce from actor Nelson Langton. She and Tolson were divorced six months ago, but a reliable source reported that he was on his way to the west coast to attempt a reconciliation at the time of the crash.

Miss Devond's other husbands were. . . .

Patrick closed the book and put it on the stack. He was interested only in Jason Tolson, and there wasn't anything else about him in the clipping or in the book. For a short while he had had a father, and now he didn't have him any more.

Uncle Darius was feeling "poorly, very poorly in-deed" the next day, so there was no work on the new scrapbook. Patrick was glad to get out of it, even at the expense of Uncle Darius' upset stomach, because he knew he would not be able to paste in the clippings without saying something about the clippings he had seen in the attic yesterday. And anything he might say would certainly be in the form of an accusation. "Why didn't you tell me my father was dead? Why didn't you tell me he was married to somebody named Bonita Devond?" Or maybe even, "What was so wrong with Jason Tolson that you won't even let Beryl and Athena mention his name to me?"

Of course, he knew the reason. There could be only one possible reason. Beryl had not been mar-ried to Jason Tolson, and she had done that thing that was so bad. He thought about Friday night and how Beryl had sat on Danton's jacket and held her arms up to him, and he wondered and won-dered. . . . Then he didn't want to think about it any more, because he was beginning to *know*, and knowledge was painful.

And yet, Beryl herself didn't seem to mind talk-ing about Jaybird. Last night he had gotten the impression that she wanted to tell him but couldn't because of Uncle Darius. Would she, he wondered, have admitted that she was his mother if she weren't afraid of Uncle Darius?

And just why in the living hell was everybody so scared of Uncle Darius?

He answered the question almost before it had finished forming in his mind. There wasn't any one thing you could put your finger on. It was simply that all of the parts of Uncle Darius added up to a total of Authority, expressed in the most authoritative way. Actually, Uncle Darius had never done many of the things he had threatened to do. He had never skinned Patrick alive; he had never taken his cane to him; he had never locked him in his room and made him eat mush for a month. But the fear of Uncle Darius was there, because Patrick nursed the notion that if seriously provoked, Uncle Darius was more than capable of carrying out to the nth degree any and every threat he had ever made. Athena and Beryl apparently realized this also, and that was why Athena was the way she was and never had any fun, and why Beryl was afraid to leave home and marry Christopher Danton. It would serve Uncle Darius right if Beryl did run away. It would be his lie about Celinda coming true at last.

Patrick spent the morning on the front porch reading and the afternoon in the woods. He was growing accustomed to the woods now—the long shadows, the strange bird calls, the different smells of the evergreens and magnolias. Even the tombstone was getting to be a familiar landmark which he hardly noticed. He wondered why he had ever been funny about the woods when he could not have found a better place to play.

At five o'clock he started to the front gate to meet Beryl. Since Uncle Darius was still poorly, he would not be going to the shop to walk home with her.

"Where are you going, Patrick?" Athena called as he went out the front door.

"To the gate to meet Beryl."

"See that you don't go any farther than that," she said. "Uncle Darius has enough on his mind without any more disobedience from you. No wonder he has an upset stomach."

"I thought it was from something he ate," Patrick said.

"Sometimes nerves can cause stomach trouble," she said. "And you have given us all a bad case of nerves lately."

"I haven't done anything bad, Athena. Honest I haven't." Except to tell a lie, he added to himself. And he wondered if that was really wrong, since things would have been a lot worse for everybody if he had told the truth.

Athena shrugged without answering, a gesture which said more clearly than words, "You're too much for me, Patrick."

He edged out the door, hesitating to see if she was going to tell him not to go. When she said nothing, he turned and ran down the walk.

Scrupulously, he stopped just inside the gate, because to put even so much as a toe on the sidewalk would be the grossest disobedience. He looked back at the house, but Athena was not on the porch, nor could he see her at any of the front windows. He leaned forward and put his right foot on the sidewalk, then hastily drew it back. "There," he said, feeling much better. After that he was content merely to peep around the gate to see if Beryl was coming.

He was so busy watching the sidewalk that he almost didn't notice the car that stopped at the curb in front of the gate. When he did look around, he recognized the car immediately, and then realized that Beryl was in it.

"Thank you, sir, for the ride," she said mockingly.

"You're welcome, ma'am," Danton said. Then, "Tell your uncle I hope his stomach keeps him in bed for a long time."

Beryl laughed. "That's not very nice."

"I'm not a very nice person."

"I'll argue that point."

"Tonight at Louis and Natalie's?" he said.

"I wish there were somewhere else we could meet," she said. "Uncle Darius has already commented that I'm wearing out my welcome over there."

"Is there anywhere else?"

"No, not when you remember they're the only ones who know about us, *and* they're willing to be our alibi, et cetera."

"And Uncle Darius doesn't know that half the time when you're supposed to be visiting Natalie you're . . ." Danton broke off and began to laugh.

"Hush, you dope. Neither does Natalie." Beryl leaned over and kissed his cheek and got out of the car. "Pick me up here at eight-thirty," she said. "I'll manage it somehow."

The car shot away and Beryl went through the gate, saw Patrick, and jumped.

"Why, Patrick, how long have you been here?"

"A long time. Waiting for you." He was also waiting to see what sort of explanation she would come up with now that she knew someone in the family had seen her with Danton.

"Mr. Danton saw me walking home and offered me a ride. I think he wanted to see if I could influence Uncle Darius about selling the property."

That was about as much explanation as she was going to make, Patrick figured. "What do you suppose Uncle Darius would say about you riding with him?" he volunteered.

"Oh, I don't think he'd mind. After all, it's only a couple of blocks."

"I'll bet he'd say you'd be better off walking a couple of blocks by yourself than riding with a Yankee," he said.

Beryl looked at him for a minute and then burst into laughter. "That's exactly, to the word, what he'd say. So maybe we'd better not tell him. This will be our little secret. Okay, Patrick?"

"Okay." He fell into step beside her as they went up the walk. "I've got lots of secrets that I'll never tell anybody."

"I'll bet you do at that," Beryl said, and then added, "Did you find out anything when you went back to the attic last night?"

"I found out that Jason Tolson died two days after the plane crash. Beryl, why didn't anybody tell me that he was dead or that he married somebody after you came back home?"

"After *I* came back home! You mean Celinda, don't you?"

"Yes, I guess that's who I mean." They were at the porch now, and he knew the conversation would end before he found out anything more. Beryl didn't seem to be in much of a truthful mood anyway, because she was going on with that Celinda stuff.

"When Celinda died, we sent Jaybird a telegram," Beryl said. "We saw in the papers a week later that he had married that Devond woman. I think that woman was the reason Cee came home anyway."

"What do you mean?" He caught at her skirt as she went up the steps, trying to hold her back.

"I'm sorry, Patrick. I've said all I can say. In fact, I've said much too much. So don't ask me any more questions, promise? You'll get me in trouble."

"Please, Beryl, I've *got* to know." There seemed to be no way he could make her understand that he would go plumb out of his head if he didn't find out these things right away.

She bent down and kissed the top of his head. "I know you do, sweetie, and one of these days when you're a little older, you will. Actually, you know it all now, except for one or two little details you're not old enough to understand, and they shouldn't bother you one way or the other. You can take my word for that. Now, let's go inside."

After supper Beryl went outside to wait for

Natalie. At least, that's what she told them. It apparently had not occurred to her that Patrick had heard her talking with Danton in the car. Patrick heard the horn blow and heard Beryl call, "Coming," and he knew the house was going to be unnaturally quiet and unbearably lonely for the rest of the evening. Uncle Darius had come down for supper and had sat at the table for a few minutes before deciding he had better go back to his room. Now Patrick and Athena sat in the living room, Patrick staring silently at the TV set, wishing he had the nerve to ask to turn it on, while Athena clipped recipes out of magazines with the occasional comment, "Perhaps I'll have Mavis try this sometime." If Beryl had been there she might have played canasta or gin with him. For a moment he resented Christopher Danton for taking Beryl away from her family. He could almost understand Uncle Darius' attitude. Unconsciously, he gave a large sigh.

"What's the matter, Patrick?" Athena asked.

"I'm dying of clotted boredom." He had heard Louis Nichols say that, and it sounded like exactly what he, Patrick, was dying of. Staying in his room for three days and then not being allowed to go out of the yard for a week was considerable punishment for a boy whose chief occupations were winning battles against terrific odds, catching dozens of cattle rustlers single-handed, and conquering monsters that would make the Frankenstein monster look about as vicious as Huckleberry Hound. But anything Uncle Darius could dish out, Patrick could take, and he would not have admitted otherwise, even to himself.

He thought Athena might have suggested turning on TV herself, or anyway have come up with something fairly amusing for him to do. But all she said was, "If you're unhappy here, then I suggest you retire."

She didn't have to be quite so uppity, he thought. "I think I will. I need to get rested up for tomorrow anyway."

"What are you planning for tomorrow?"

Not a blessed thing, of course, but she had taken the bait nicely. He gave her an enigmatic smile and said, "Good night, Athena," and left the room before she could question him further.

It was much later—but he didn't know how much—when he awoke suddenly and sat up in bed. Probably Beryl had just come in and that was what awakened him. He lay back down, but the noise came again. The sound of voices beneath his window. For just a minute or two he lay very still, letting the disembodied voices float upward to his window as though transported on a whipped cream cloud. The cloud was wafted through the window and settled over his bed, the words the voices said lost in layers of fluffy fog which could not, of itself, disperse in the warm, still, summer air.

And then he was wide awake, wondering who was talking under his window. He jumped out of bed and knelt at the window seat, pressing his forehead against the screen. There was a full moon and it was almost as bright as day outside. He saw the two of them instantly, not right under his window after all, but standing at the edge of the clearing. Danton had his arm around Beryl.

"It's this way," she was saying. "After you see, I think you'll understand better how things are—have always been with us."

She moved out of the circle of his arm, took his hand, and led him toward the woods.

Patrick was out of his room almost before Beryl had finished speaking, his bare feet padding down the stairs like a cat stalking a bird, through the back hall and kitchen and out to the back porch. He left the kitchen door unlocked so there would be no question this time of having to wake up everybody to get in.

The dewy, squishy grass felt good as he ran silently across the clearing. At the edge of the woods, he stopped. It was darker under all those trees, and he might get lost. But he did not dare go back for his flashlight, because then Danton and Beryl would see him for sure. His confidence somewhat shaken, he ventured forth anyway. Surely he had been in the woods enough recently to know every tree, every stone, and every clump of moss by heart. If Beryl and Danton could find their way, he could keep up with them—or rather, keep a few steps behind them.

They had a head start, and he was almost to where he thought the tombstone was before he caught the sound of their voices again. He could not tell what they were saying, but heard Beryl's soft laughter, and then a serious note changed the tone of her voice. Why was it, he wondered, that people's voices did not sound the same in summer as they did in winter? In summer, voices seemed to hang in the air the way Beryl's and Danton's had a few minutes ago when they had first awakened him: mysterious, beautiful with the clarity of tiny bells. And if the voices could have a color, they would be silver. In winter it was completely different. Voices didn't float. They plodded along slowly, and though they had a ring to them, it was not the tone of tiny bells, but more like the clanging of the big bell in the belfry over at First Methodist. Winter voices were not as transparent as summer voices, and they had a heavier color—gold, maybe.

Patrick liked the silver voices better, and he walked faster to get nearer to Beryl and Danton. He wasn't sure, but he thought they must be very close to the back of the Quincannon property, not too far from the tombstone, except that by his calculation they would have to bear more to the left if that were where they were going.

"It should be right around here somewhere," he heard Beryl saying. "What we need is a flashlight."

Patrick silently seconded the motion.

"If I weren't already convinced that your uncle is crazy, this would do it," Danton said.

Not really crazy, Patrick thought. Just screwy as hell, is all.

"Eccentric, yes," said Beryl, "but not crazy. I think we came too far down this way. Let's go up here a bit, where the little clearing is. It's at least brighter there."

They picked their way across misshappen tree

roots and underbrush, stalked by Patrick Quincannon Tolson, Boy Sleuth. He wondered if Beryl
would be able to see the patchwork moss on the
grave, and if she, like Uncle Darius, would think it
had been done by moles.

"Here it is, just ahead," Beryl said. "See the
stone?"

"My God, you were serious! It really is here. I
thought this was some kind of joke."

"Hardly anything I'd joke about."

They were standing beside the stone, and Patrick
stopped behind the trunk of a giant oak.

"What does it say on the stone?" Danton asked.
"I can't quite make it out."

"Celinda, Beloved Daughter of Donald and Sarah
Quincannon. *Requiescat in Pace.*"

Danton laughed. "Rest in peace, that's ironic
enough. Does everybody know there's no one
buried here?"

"No one—except the family and Mavis—knows
that the stone is here. It was purely a whim of
Uncle Darius', and certainly Athena and I weren't
quick to rush all over town telling everybody that
our uncle had put up a tombstone behind the
house."

"You said that after I saw, I'd understand better
how things are," he said. "The fact is, I understand
less now than I did before. To me, this," he
gestured toward the stone, "would be all the more
reason to leave this place. Instead, it seems to bind
you to it. This is ridiculous, Beryl, and if you can't
see that, then you're as . . ." He stopped.

"As crazy as my uncle? That's what you were going to say, isn't it?"

Danton did not answer.

"Please, won't you even *try* to understand?"

"I'm exhausted from trying. You say you can't leave now but later you can. How is anything going to be changed later—and how much later did you have in mind? Your staying on in this setting is incomprehensible to me."

There was something like a whimper from Beryl. "I'm not as strong as you are, Chris. I don't have the guts to walk out. I keep thinking of what happened in the past when somebody defied Uncle Darius, and I'm afraid to set that kind of thing in motion."

"But this time you wouldn't be there to feel the force of it."

"Patrick would," Beryl said quietly. "Don't you see—"

"No, I don't," said Danton, "You're not his mother. Besides, you wouldn't have to desert him. Briarman's Cliff isn't so far that you couldn't see Patrick every day if you wanted to. You *can* have a car again, you know."

"He's such a little boy. So vulnerable somehow. You know, Chris, I think Rusty Nichols and I are his only contacts with reality during the summer. Living here, the way we do, is like being in a world that doesn't really exist and—I don't know—but I've always had a feeling, even when Patrick was a baby, that someone with a grasp on reality should stay near him to keep him from being oversheltered and growing up with a completely wrong idea of what the world outside the iron gates is like."

"Beryl, for God's sake, you're not saying you think we should wait to get married until Patrick grows up, are you? I think you've got an obsession about that kid, and you're just going to have to get over it."

"No, I'm not saying wait that long. But I am saying that he's had a strange life, stranger even than he realizes now, and one of these days—soon, it's already happening—he's going to realize that the Quincannons aren't like other people. He's going to need someone around who can be a shock absorber for him."

"You're overdramatizing things, Beryl. Kids can take the licks, mental and physical, much better than adults can."

"Patrick isn't like most children, Chris. He's never had a chance to be."

"Maybe not, but all kids have certain things in common." There was a pause, then, "I'm not going to argue this point—any of these points—with you any more, Beryl. I've about had it—up to here. If you decide you want to—and can—break away from what you consider insurmountable obstacles, okay, fine. But you'll have to come to me and tell me so. I won't bring up the subject again—ever."

"*Please*, Chris. Don't make me have to choose between—"

"I can't help being the way I am. And I don't suppose you can help being the way you are."

Beryl reached across the tombstone and put her hands on his face. Patrick leaned farther out from behind the tree.

"I don't think you love me, Chris."

Danton went around the stone and put his arms around her, urging her gently to the patchwork moss. As Patrick saw him kissing her, he felt his face grow hot. There was something terribly embarrassing about watching this sort of thing, even though no one knew he was watching. He supposed that was why he hadn't really watched them that night from the car when they went across the cliff.

They were lying down on the moss now, so close together that in the darkness it was impossible to tell where one body stopped and another began.

"Chris, stop! For heaven's sake, not here." Beryl seemed to be trying to pull away, but Danton did not let her go very far. Maybe a couple of inches.

"Why not here? I think this is a splendid place."

"*No*, we can't here. Not right beside the stone. . . ."

"But you said yourself nobody's buried here. This isn't a cemetery, Beryl. Are you going to start arguing about that, too?"

Beryl did not protest any more, and Danton was leaning over her as though he would never let her up while the world stood. As their bodies merged into one shadow again, Patrick left the oak tree and fled through the woods, cutting his feet on small stones, scratching his legs on the underbrush, running, running, as though terror gave him sight in the darkness. Faster, faster, something inside him was crying, and he whipped himself on like a jockey in a race, faster, faster, toward the familiar safety of the house.

**13**

It was three weeks after the visit of Father Conroy to the Quincannon house before Patrick went to find the priest. The first week had been the week of Patrick's imprisonment, and for two weeks after that he didn't have time to give much thought to Father Conroy and the "choice." The truth was, he completely forgot about the priest's visit until a hot afternoon in the middle of July when he was on his way home from Rusty's and saw Father Conroy on the other side of the street. He didn't have time to stop then; Athena had told him to be home by five, but tomorrow morning for sure he would go to see the priest.

It took him completely by surprise that he had forgotten about Father Conroy's visit. Usually, he never forgot anything, not even the smallest, least important things. But lately there had been so much to think about, so many things he had never thought about before—some he hoped he'd never have to think about again—that his mind had been wholly occupied on all levels. It seemed that before he had time to select one new thought, the outcome of a new experience or an overheard conversation, from a massive array of new thoughts, time to sort and file it in his memory according to its importance, there was something else demanding his immediate attention. The result was, his mind was like a neglected office where mail and documents have piled up too rapidly to be put away in their proper places.

The following morning, as soon as he finished helping Uncle Darius with the paste-ups, he left the house, looking over his shoulder guiltily several times (if Uncle Darius *could* by any chance read his thoughts and know that he was going to see the priest, he might find himself spending the whole, entire summer inside that blessed iron fence).

If you want to get away with something, don't sneak to do it; do it openly. That was what Louis Nichols had told Rusty the time he had caught him sneaking into the movie when Rusty had been told positively that he could not go because he was already overextended on his credit. Patrick thought about the advice now and walked boldly down the sidewalk toward the Catholic rectory. Anyone looking at him would surely think he was on a righteous errand for all the world to see, and no one would ever guess that if he got caught he would be skinned alive, maybe even buried alive in the pseudo-grave in the back yard.

The rectory, a graystone building like the church, was beside the church, but set back so far from the sidewalk that you were almost right in front of it before you saw it. Behind the rectory and church, taking up the rest of the block, was the Catholic cemetery. Patrick had never seen the cemetery close up (like his own yard, it was fenced in, with ivy growing on the fence), but whenever he looked through the ivy, it appeared to be a very fascinating place. He had never seen so many statues in his life. From what he could see, it looked as though every single grave had a statue of some kind on it or beside it.

Once, when he was a little boy and had just begun to notice the differences in certain people and places, he had asked Uncle Darius why the Catholics were not buried in Laurelton Cemetery along with everybody else and the answer he got was, "Protestant dirt isn't good enough for them." Patrick hadn't understood this at the time (still didn't, for that matter), but he'd supposed by the same token that Protestant dirt wasn't good enough for the mythical Celinda either, since her tombstone had been placed in the back yard instead of the cemetery. This was, of course, at the time when he thought there was a Celinda and that she was buried in Quincannon dirt in the back yard.

Still walking confidently, although he was beginning to quake inside, Patrick went up the rectory walk. He hesitated only briefly before ringing the bell. He didn't really know what in the world he would say when Father Conroy came to the door, but his Sunday school lesson at First Methodist last Sunday had been about how "God will provide," and he figured if God was so good at providing, He could provide a few words along with the other essentials of life. He said a quick prayer to that effect in case God didn't happen to be giving Patrick His full attention right that minute. (He just might be so busy watching a sparrow fall out of a tree that He had momentarily forgotten all about Patrick and his difficulties.) His Sunday school teacher had said that praying was just the same as direct dialing to God, and this botched up Patrick's whole, entire picture of heaven. Now when he imagined the long, golden streets, he had to ruin the vision by sticking up crummy black telephone poles along the shining route.

Father Conroy seemed in no hurry to answer the door, so Patrick rang the bell again. He could hear it chiming in the back part of the house, and there was no other sound. Father Conroy was probably downtown—or maybe in the church.

Patrick went slowly across the grassy lawn which connected the rectory and the church. He was almost tiptoeing, his former bravado on leave of absence. He stopped in front of the massive double doors and tugged gently at one, hoping to find it locked. But the door opened surprisingly easily, and he slipped inside, standing for a minute in the dim vestibule.

At first, all he could see was the little red light glowing in the lanternlike thing near the altar, then his eyes became accustomed to the cool semi-darkness of the church. The statues seemed almost like people staring at him, waiting to see what he was going to do. He took a few steps down the aisle, then stopped and sat down in the nearest pew.

Father Conroy was not in the church, and in a way, it was a relief not to find him there. Patrick looked around him, noticing things which had escaped his attention when he was there before: the sort-of-but-not-quite pictures along the walls from the altar rail to the back of the church (the one nearest him showed Jesus going up a hill, almost falling beneath the weight of the cross); the corner where a rack was filled with tiny candles (three were burning); the little benches beneath the pews which could be pulled out and, he supposed, knelt upon if you wanted to pray to the statues.

After a while, the strangeness of the church began to wear off and he did not feel quite so much like an alien in a foreign land. He was not in some faraway never-never land, he told himself, but sitting in a church right in Laurelton, not more than five blocks from home. The statues looked less forbidding—if you really looked at them closely, their expressions were kind of friendly. In fact, if he could think of anything to pray about, he wouldn't mind pulling out one of the little benches and kneeling on it. But there wasn't one single thing he could ask God for. The things that had happened to him had been definite and final, and there was no way they could be undone by praying. God couldn't, for instance, suddenly decree that there *had* been a Celinda and that she was buried in the back yard and that everything was the way Uncle Darius said it was and no one had lied to him. There was *one* thing, though, that God might help with.

He pulled out the bench, knelt, and whispered, "Please, God, let Beryl have the guts to run away with Christopher Danton before something bad happens to her. Don't let her think she's got to stay with Athena and Uncle Darius because of me."

As he sat down again and pushed the bench back under the pew in front, he felt his face burning. He should not have, after all, prayed for what he did.

Something bad *already* was happening to Beryl which maybe God hadn't noticed yet, and he had just called God's attention to it by praying about it. No matter what he did, he seemed to have a real talent for messing up Beryl's life—starting with being born.

He stood up, shoved his hands into his pockets, and walked out of the church. In front of the church he turned toward the corner, ready to go home, but he stopped as he heard his name called.

"Patrick, over here." Father Conroy, standing in front of the rectory, was waving to him. He walked slowly across the lawn to meet the priest.

"I saw you as you came out of church," Father Conroy said. "I am so glad you . . ." He hesitated as though not quite sure what to say.

"I was looking for you and I went to your house, but you weren't there so I thought you might be in church."

"I was downtown on some errands. Won't you come in and visit me now, Patrick?"

"I—I . . . Yes, I guess so, thank you." It was funny, when he looked at the priest he found it impossible not to see the large nose, and yet he didn't really *think* about the nose as he stared at it. He wondered if it would make Father Conroy feel any better about the almost misshapen feature if he told him this, but then he decided maybe the priest didn't feel too bad about it anyway, and besides, there were other things to talk about.

"Come in," Father Conroy said. "We'll stir up some lemonade. I'm delighted to see you, Patrick." He paused momentarily, then added, "I suppose Mr. Quincannon has no idea where you are?"

"Not the first idea in the world," Patrick said. "And I'd be much obliged if you wouldn't tell him."

The priest nodded and led the way into the rectory, through the living room to a screened porch which looked out on the back of the church and part of the cemetery.

"It will be cooler out here," he said. "Sit down, Patrick. I'll just get the lemonade and join you in a minute."

Patrick sat down on a bright green glider. If he were going to be a preacher, he thought, he would never be a Catholic one, because they must get terribly lonely staying by themselves all the time. It might even be better to live with someone you didn't like than to live alone.

Beryl had said once that people who lived by themselves got peculiar. But then, as he thought about it now, sometimes people who lived with other people were peculiar, too, so what was the difference?

Father Conroy returned and handed him a tall frosted glass. "Maybe this will cut the heat by a few degrees," he said.

Patrick thanked him, took a sip from the glass, and then blurted out suddenly, "I said a prayer while I was in the church. Do you think since I'm not a Catholic that God heard me?"

"Yes, Patrick, He heard you."

"Will it come true?"

"You speak of your prayer as though it were a wish, Patrick. Wishes come true, or don't come true, and prayers are granted . . ."

"Or not granted," he said quickly.

"It is a common mistake," Father Conroy said. "Most people offer their prayers with the same amount of confidence they would have in saying 'Star bright, star light, first star I see tonight.'"

"Do you think my prayer will be granted?"

"If God thinks it right that it should be."

This wasn't what Patrick considered a definite answer, but at that, it was as definite as anything he had heard over at First Methodist. He began to rock the glider slowly back and forth as he looked toward the cemetery and wondered what the difference was in Catholic and Protestant dirt. He thought about asking the priest, but changed his mind. He had come to ask what Father Conroy had meant when he said Patrick had a choice.

Father Conroy, noticing the direction of Patrick's stare, said, "Have you ever been to your mother's grave, Patrick?"

"Lots of times," he said. "How did you know about the grave?"

The priest gave him a puzzled look. "How did I know about . . . I don't understand you, Patrick."

"I thought nobody knew about it but Uncle Darius, Athena, Beryl, Mavis, and me. At least that's what I heard Beryl tell somebody. Oh, yes, that somebody Beryl told knows about it now. And you know, the funny thing is, we all know nobody's buried there, but none of us will say it out loud. They don't know I know about it, though. Except Mavis, she knows."

"I'm afraid you've lost me, Patrick."

Now Patrick was the one who was puzzled.

"I guess you don't know about it after all. If you'll promise not to tell, I'll tell you."

The priest nodded.

"Cross your heart and hope to die?"

"Cross my heart and hope to die," Father Conroy said.

"It's in the woods behind our house. Uncle Darius put up a tombstone back there for somebody named Celinda who was supposed to be my mother, only I dug the grave up and there's nobody buried there and—you know what?—there never was anybody named Celinda. They didn't want me to know who my real mother was, so they made up this Celinda person."

Father Conroy was shaking his head, the way Uncle Darius did sometimes when he thought Patrick was telling him the biggest lie in the whole, entire world.

"Patrick, Patrick," he said softly. "It's worse than I thought. Much worse."

"What's worse? I'm telling you the gospel truth, Father Conroy, and if you don't want to believe it. . . ."

Father Conroy stood up suddenly. "Haven't they told you anything at all about your mother?" He was looking at Patrick as though he felt very sorry for him. "For years I've wondered what to do about you, Patrick. I've thought and prayed about it, but I never found the answer until you came into the church a few weeks ago. I think God sent you to me, but even then I wasn't sure what I should do, and therefore I let you go away with nothing. Now I have been given a second chance and I think God means for me to use it as I think best."

Patrick drew back on the glider, his eyes wide. "You mean you're going to make me a Catholic before I know what hits me?" The mental image of Uncle Darius' face loomed large.

"You are a Catholic, Patrick," Father Conroy said quietly.

"I'm a Methodist," Patrick said instantly. "Uncle Darius and Athena and Beryl—all of us are Methodists."

"Come with me," Father Conroy said. "I want to show you something."

Reluctantly, Patrick followed the priest off the porch and along a path which led to the small cemetery. There was no escape now. If Father Conroy hadn't already hexed all the Methodist out of him and made him turn Catholic, it was only a matter of minutes. Strangely enough, it did not now seem to be the worst fate that could befall him. Father Conroy was very nice—nicer, in fact, every time Patrick saw him.

They walked among the graves and Patrick stared at the statues. There was one of the Virgin Mary almost exactly like the one in church, only smaller; there was one of a shepherd holding a little lamb; another tombstone had just a lone lamb on top. There were more crosses than Patrick could count.

"Here we are," Father Conroy said, stopping beside a grave. There was no statue here, only a marble marker, very similar to the one in Patrick's back yard.

He read the words on the stone out loud. "Celinda Quincannon Tolson, January 28, 1939–March 16, 1958."

He read the words again, silently this time, then whistled between his teeth. "Gooo-oood night! There must be tombstones with her name on them all over town."

"No, Patrick, I think not," Father Conroy said. "I was under the impression that this was the only one until you told me about the other."

"Seems to me like a lot of trouble to go to for somebody that was made up. Did Uncle Darius put this one here, too?"

"No, your Aunt Athena and your Aunt Beryl put this one here. This is where your mother is buried, Patrick." He added with a small smile, "And I'd appreciate it if you wouldn't dig up the grave this time."

"But—but . . ." He was about to say, Beryl is my mother. "But there wasn't a Celinda. They just made her up."

"There *was* a Celinda."

"Did you ever see her with your own eyes?"

"Many times."

"Cross your heart and hope to die?"

"Cross my heart and hope to die."

"Was she really my mother?"

"Yes, of course."

"Then why . . ." Patrick sat down on the grass beside the grave. "Why is she buried here instead of in our back yard where Uncle Darius said she was?"

"Has he ever actually *said* she was buried there, Patrick?"

"Well no, I guess not in so many words, but the tombstone and all. . . ."

"I think I can understand that," Father Conroy said. He sat down beside Patrick.

Patrick remembered suddenly why he had come to see the priest. "You came to see Uncle Darius not long ago and I heard you say something about a choice. Did it have anything to do with—with my mother and me?"

"Yes, it did."

"What kind of choice were you talking about?"

Father Conroy sighed and looked at all the statues and tombstones as though he didn't really see them. "Patrick, doesn't anyone in your family ever talk to you or answer your questions and tell you the things you want to know?"

"Mavis used to, but she chickened out because she's scared of Uncle Darius, I think. Beryl does sometimes, but she doesn't talk too much. Uncle Darius and Athena don't have too much to say."

"Patrick, I think you should hear about your mother from someone close to her—probably Beryl. And when she has told you, then I want you to come back to me and I'll explain to you about the 'choice' then." There was a grim look on his face, and the tip of his huge nose seemed to have dropped almost to his upper lip.

"But I've asked Beryl about a hundred times . . ."

"Tell her you have been here. This time I think she'll tell you what you want to know." He stood up. "Come now. Let's go back and finish the lemonade, and then you can scoot home and get a lot of things straight that I'm sure have been bothering you."

Patrick walked a few steps behind the priest, turning before they had gone very far to look at the second Celinda tombstone one more time.

He had no difficulty getting Beryl alone that night so he could talk to her. She seldom went out after supper now. In fact, since that night he had followed her and Danton into the woods, Beryl had been out only twice at night, and both times she had gotten into Natalie's car. He knew this because he had watched from the porch.

When it was his bedtime, he said good night, and as he was leaving the room he motioned for Beryl to follow him. He waited for her at the foot of the steps.

"I want to talk to you," he whispered. "How long before you'll be up?"

"Just a few minutes," she whispered back. "Shall I come to your room?"

"No, Athena might hear us. I'll wait in your room."

By the time he had had his bath and plunked himself down in the middle of Beryl's big bed, she came in. "What now, Patrick? What sort of hobgoblins are chasing you this time?"

"I saw Celinda's grave today," he said.

"Oh—you went walking in the woods?"

"I went walking in the Catholic cemetery with Father Conroy." He watched the many changes in her face while this information was digested. "Father Conroy told me to come home and talk to you and then to go back to talk to him again."

"He had no right to tell you anything!" Beryl said, her face turning red with anger.

"Did *he* promise Uncle Darius, too?"

"No, but . . ."

"Well, he didn't tell me much of anything. He said you would."

Beryl sighed. "Come to think of it, I suppose he had as much right to tell you as we had *not* to tell you. What do you want to know, Patrick?" She sat down on the bed beside him.

"About my mother."

"What do you want to know about her?"

"Everything."

Beryl was silent for a long time. Then she pulled a pillow from beneath the spread, propped it against the headboard, and leaned against it. "All right, Patrick, I guess there are some things more important than a promise made to Uncle Darius years ago. I'll tell you as much as I know about Cee—and since we were alike in some ways, I suppose I knew her better than anyone else. Which isn't to say that I always understood her.

"Celinda was only a year old when. . . ."

Beryl hesitated for so long that Patrick thought she had changed her mind about telling him what was what—or rather, who was who. Just as he was about to urge her on, she said, "Patrick, you really don't know anything about this family, do you?"

He decided against letting her in on the secret that he had found out the most important bit of information about the family, namely that it was screwy as hell. "I guess not," he said finally, and braced himself to hear the history of the Quincannons, probably dating to the maiden voyage of the Mayflower.

"Celinda was only a year old when our parents were killed in an automobile accident," Beryl said, and Patrick heaved a small sigh of relief that she was taking up where she left off. "Only Athena can really remember those first days when our lives changed so radically, but I have vague memories of the strangeness, the people coming and going, Mavis crying as though the world had ended. . . ."

Patrick lay on his stomach, his chin cupped in his hands, his eyes never leaving Beryl's face. She had a sort of dreamy look now, he thought. As though she weren't talking to him at all, as though she had forgotten he was here and was just remembering out loud.

"When Donald and Sarah—our parents, your grandparents, Patrick—were married, Uncle Darius moved out of this house and went to live in a boarding house. But after the accident, there was no question but that he would move back. There was no one else to take care of us, and besides, the house was half his anyway. It had belonged to him and our father jointly, and of course our father's half was left to the three of us and Uncle

Darius was our guardian. I've often wondered what Uncle Darius thought about taking on the guardianship of three small girls, but that was one of the few things about which I never heard him express an opinion.

"On the day of the funeral, Uncle Darius moved back into his old room and told Mavis he would double her salary if she would sleep at the house to help him with his three charges at night, but she told him she had to go to her own home at night. So he said to Athena, 'You're going to have to help me with your sisters. I don't know much about children, especially little girls.' Athena took Uncle Darius as seriously as he had intended her to, and began to act like a second mother to Cee and me. With both Uncle Darius and Athena representing authority, this brought Cee and me closer and closer together, and put a barrier between us and Athena."

Beryl's eyes focused on him suddenly; her voice sharpened. "Oh Patrick, what can I tell you about your mother? If only I can tell you so you'll feel you really knew her—as a person and not just as the heroine of some half-forgotten story. . . ."

Patrick didn't say anything, afraid of disturbing Beryl's train of thought. To distract her now was the last thing he wanted to do.

"From the time she was a small child, Celinda had a knack for sizing up a person or a situation and going right to the core of a matter," she said. "When she was twelve, I remember overhearing her say to Athena, 'You know what's your trouble, Athena? You have absolutely no sense of humor.'

Sometimes I was convinced that Cee felt things more strongly than other people, was aware of everything on levels where others' minds never went."

Beryl smiled slightly. "When Celinda was good, she was, as Mavis said, an angel, but when she was bad, her temper was enough to cause storm warnings to be hoisted all over Laurel County. 'She has a high point of emotionalism,' was the way Uncle Darius explained it. And yet, in spite of the fact that she caused him more concern than Athena or even I ever could, she was always his favorite. He tolerated Athena and me, but he adored Celinda.

"But so did Athena and I. She was such a lovely child. Blonde with big brown eyes. And she had a way of looking at the world as though it had been created for the sole purpose of being looked at and enjoyed and tasted and touched and lived in by one Celinda Quincannon."

Her face darkened. "She had her first run-in with Uncle Darius when she was nine years old. She told me about it later—the part I didn't see for myself.

"Uncle Darius was standing at the window of his office in the bank when he saw Celinda walking home from school with a boy—and the boy was carrying her books. Uncle Darius went to the front door of the bank and called her. 'You may go along, young man,' he said to the boy, 'Celinda will be with me for a while.' 'Oh no,' Celinda said, 'Joey is going to buy me a sundae before we go home.' Uncle Darius pulled Celinda inside the door, not caring about the watching tellers and customers, and said, 'Celinda, you are to wait until that boy leaves and then you are to go straight home. You are too young to be running around with boys.'

"'I'm not running around,' Celinda said. 'I'm just going to eat a sundae with Joey and then he's walking me home.'

"'And in the future, you are to walk home alone, unless accompanied by another girl,' Uncle Darius continued.

"Celinda stared at him and then said in her calm, reasonable voice, 'All of the boys walk home with their best girls, and I'm Joey's best girl. You'd just better be glad the boys don't think I'm a drip like—'

"'Celinda!' Uncle Darius thundered, 'I have said all I'm going to say on the subject. You are to go *straight* home, and alone.'

"'Nuts!' Celinda said loudly enough to cause eyes to look in her direction from every grilled window. 'You don't know what you're talking about.'"

Beryl was clearly amused at this part of her story. "Can you imagine what it was like? The sight of Darius Quincannon, president of the Laurelton bank, being told off by his nine-year-old niece!"

Patrick giggled. "He hasn't changed much, has he? I guess he was always the way he is now."

"Celinda left the bank and rejoined Joey in the next block," Beryl said. "And when Uncle Darius got home that afternoon his first words were, 'Well, Celinda?'

"Celinda gave him one of her angelic smiles. 'Joey treated me to a hot fudge sundae,' she said. 'Did you ever eat one, Uncle D.?'

"'Celinda, you disobeyed me.' His voice was sterner than I'd ever heard it at that time.

"'I guess I did,' she said, 'but there's very little harm in a hot fudge sundae.'

"In spite of himself, Uncle Darius laughed, but then he said, 'You may go to your room and you may not leave it until tomorrow morning. I will not tolerate disobedience from any of my nieces. And until you are of age, I had better not hear of any more boys walking you home after school.'

"I remember Athena and I listened to this exchange from the living room, and we stared at each other in amazement. This was the first time Cee had ever been punished by Uncle Darius."

"Eating a hot fudge sundae wasn't anything to get punished for," Patrick said hotly. "But it sounds just like Uncle Darius. That's him all over."

Beryl gave him an indulgent smile, as though he had missed the whole point, but he ignored this and asked, "Did Joey whoever-he-was walk home with her again?"

"I think probably every boy in school walked home with Cee at one time or another," Beryl said. "I remember Mavis saying once, 'I declare, one of these days I'm going to have to sweep Miss Cee's boy friends off the steps so she can come in and eat her supper.' She was very popular, there was no question about that. And through the years Uncle Darius watched, more or less silently, as the boys came and went from the house. The only times he raised serious objections were the few times Cee broke the nine-thirty curfew."

Beryl's eyes had a faraway look again and her face clouded. "That was the cause of her first tantrum."

Patrick drew in his breath in surprise. For the first time he pictured his mother—that angel, as described by Mavis—as a human being who enjoyed hot fudge sundaes, disobeyed authority occasionally, allied herself with Beryl against Athena and Uncle Darius (this was the part about her he understood best). But real honest-to-goodness tantrums? This was the part he couldn't believe. Even he knew better than to try to get away with a tantrum in *this* family.

"It was the night before the junior-senior prom," Beryl said. "Uncle Darius, Athena, and I were sitting in the living room waiting for Cee to come in and model her new dress for us. And when she came in she looked like a delicate butterfly. It was a long, pale yellow dress, and her hair was a shade or two lighter than the dress. She stood in front of Uncle Darius and curtsied. 'You like?' He didn't say a word, just sat in his big chair and stared and stared. His eyes narrowed until they were hardly more than slits in a high forehead, and his face turned so purple that I thought he was holding his breath. Finally he said, 'With whom are you going to the party?'

" 'Lester Barden,' she said.

"The expression on Uncle Darius' face said clearly, 'He's not good enough for you. None of them are good enough for you,' but what he actually said was, 'You are to be home by ten o'clock.'

"'Ten o'clock!' Celinda wailed. 'You're kidding, Uncle D. You're making a funny.'

"'I am being very lenient,' Uncle Darius said. 'Nine-thirty is the usual hour. Remember, you're only fifteen.'

"'But this is the junior-senior prom,' she cried. 'Nobody will leave before midnight, and only the drips who don't have dates will leave that early.'

"'I'm not going to say it again, Celinda,' Uncle Darius said, and then he said it again. 'Ten o'clock.'

"Celinda let out a piercing scream, scaring us all speechless, and then she ran to the end table beside the sofa and picked up an oriental vase that had belonged to our mother. She took aim and threw it against the fireplace, smashing it into a thousand pieces. Then she picked up the nearest object—a lamp—and was about to smash it to the floor when Uncle Darius jumped to his feet suddenly and caught both her wrists in his hands. It was like watching a wrestling match to see him trying to get the lamp away from her. But he didn't save it. She managed to drop it on the hearth. Then she began to kick Uncle Darius in the shins, and she had her head down ready to sink her teeth into his fingers when he finally got enough of a grip on her arms to force her back to the sofa. Even while he pushed her down among the cushions, she was still kicking and trying to bite him. When he had her pinned down so she couldn't move, she burst into tears. And that, in itself, was unusual enough, for none of us had ever seen Celinda cry like that before, not even when she was a baby.

" 'Go to your room,' Uncle Darius said. 'Go to your room right now and take off that dress.'

"Celinda stopped crying and rose from the sofa as calmly as though she were awakening from an afternoon nap. She walked regally to the door, turned and looked back at us, then looked at the matching lamp on the other end table. 'One is no good without the other,' she said. She raised the lamp slowly and let it fall to the floor. Uncle Darius was so stunned he couldn't do anything but stare at her as though she had completely lost her mind."

"I guess he didn't let her out of the house again for a month or two," Patrick said.

"No mention of her wild behavior was made the next day," Beryl said, "and she went to the dance."

"And came home by ten, I'll bet," Patrick said.

"No, it was after midnight. Uncle Darius was waiting in the front hall for her, but he didn't say one word about her being late. He asked if she had had a good time, and she said of course and kissed him on the cheek and gave him a look as though she thought her Uncle Darius was the darlingest old fuddy-duddy who ever lived."

Suddenly the expression on Beryl's face scared Patrick. She was looking at the wall somewhere above his head and he realized her words now were not for him, but were part of her memories. "As for what Uncle Darius thought of Celinda—I was beginning to give a great deal of thought to that. Although I wasn't as pretty or as popular as Cee, I had my share of dates. And even Athena went out occasionally to make a fourth for bridge or to fill in when an extra man was invited to a party. But Uncle Darius never rang a curfew on us, or stared at our young men as though he detested them. But there was this strange possessiveness where Celinda was concerned. His attitude toward her was unnatur . . . no, I won't say that. His attitude was not quite normal, certainly not what you would expect from Uncle Darius. Celinda was the sun in his world, and the moon and stars, too.

"On Cee's sixteenth birthday, two weeks after the tantrum, Uncle Darius gave her a shiny red convertible, and he presented it to her almost timidly, as though he expected his gift to be rejected. The car was sitting in the driveway in front of the house when Cee went out on her way to school.

"'Whose car?' she called.

"'Yours—if you want it.' Uncle Darius said. 'Happy birthday, Celinda.'

"Athena and I were as surprised as Cee—maybe even more so. 'Well, I never!' Athena said, and Uncle Darius heard her and said, 'This will give her something to think about besides boys.' But it didn't work out that way."

Beryl was quiet for a long time, so quiet that Patrick finally said softly, "What happened then?"

Still she was quiet, apparently not hearing his question, then she said as though continuing her thoughts uninterruptedly, "After the first tantrum, the others came easier for Cee, though certainly no easier for those who observed them, and always they were brought on by something Uncle Darius did or said. Mavis said, after they were over, 'It's all part of growing up. She'll get over her fits.' And

Athena said, 'I think there must be something seriously wrong with her, Mavis. Neither Beryl nor I ever acted that way.' To which Mavis replied, 'Miss Cee is different from you-all.' And Athena agreed, 'She certainly is.'

"I was the one who decided to have a talk with her after the worst, and most destructive, of her tantrums," Beryl said. "For weeks her sunny, loving disposition had caused us all to forget that there was sometimes another side to her. And then, one night at dinner, she mentioned that she was filling out her application for Duke.

"'Duke?' Uncle Darius said. 'Duke who? What are you talking about?'

"'Duke University,' she said. 'I'm going there next year.'

"'Indeed you're not,' Uncle Darius said. 'Don't be ridiculous, Celinda.'

"And that started it all. The question of college had never come up with Athena or me. It was understood that Athena could not go to college and leave Cee and me to fend for ourselves, and I never really had any desire to go.

"Uncle Darius talked persuasively while Celinda sat and looked at him, her attention intense. There was no need for her to go to college, he told her, because there was enough money so she would never have to earn a living, and besides, colleges were not what they used to be. There were all kinds of bad influences to corrupt young people now. Peculiar ideas advocated by the professors, who were about three-fourths Communist anyway, and the other fourth so eccentric that they belonged in the state asylum. She would be much better off staying at home where she belonged.

"At the end of his lengthy discourse, Celinda said quietly, as though the subject had not been brought up before, 'I am going to college.'

"'You are not, and we'll hear no more about it,' Uncle Darius said, as though he had put a definite end to the discussion.

"In a way, he had. Cee did not say another word. She stood up beside her chair, picked up the dishes one by one from the table, even those containing food, and hurled them against the wall. All of us were too shocked to move or speak. It was like watching a scene in a movie. Food splattered across the wall and then on the floor, along with bits and pieces of china. Mavis, hearing the noise from the kitchen, rushed into the room, wiping her hands on her apron as she almost fell through the swinging door.

"'Jesus God, Miss Cee! What you doing?'

"Celinda, about to throw another dish, stopped suddenly, put the dish on the table and laughed. 'Gee, you look funny, Mavis. You ought to see your expression.' Then she left the room and went upstairs.

"That night I went to her room. 'He won't change his mind, Cee,' I said. 'You know it and I know it, so there's no need in your carrying on the way you do. You might as well forget about college.'

"'I know it. I knew it even before I mentioned it,' she said. 'At least, I *felt* it.'

"'Then why did you throw that fit? It didn't help anything.'

" 'It helped me.'

" 'How could acting like a two-year-old spoiled brat help you?'

" 'I don't know, Berrie, it just did. Sometimes things start building up inside me and they build and build until I can't stand it any more, and the only way I can tear it all down is to break things. *That's* how it helps.'

" 'What is the something that builds up? Nerves?'

" 'No, disillusionment, I think,' she said.

" 'Disillusionment in what?'

" 'The people I love.' She leaned back against the headboard of her bed and closed her eyes. 'I'd give anything if I weren't the way I am. I wish I didn't expect so much of people. You see, Berrie, I put people on pedestals—not everyone, but the people I like or *want* to like—and they always fall off the pedestals with a loud, horrible crash. But they aren't the ones who are shattered by the fall, I am. It hurts me so much that sometimes I think I can't stand it. And it goes on hurting for a long, long time. The older I get, the worse it is.'

"I thought about it for a long time, but I couldn't think of anything to say to her, nothing either wise or comforting. And I wondered then when it was that Uncle Darius had first fallen from his Celinda-made pedestal."

Beryl's eyes left that spot on the wall above his head now, but he had a feeling that she still wasn't seeing him, wasn't even aware of his presence.

"Mavis always said that when Cee was a child she bounced, when she was a young girl she bubbled, and when she became a young lady 'she went off somewhere so nobody could find her,' and this was long before Celinda actually did go away," she said.

"What Mavis meant was that she withdrew from the exterior world and went to live in an interior world where she allowed no trespassers. Outwardly she was the same, our own beautiful Celinda now become perfect, because what Athena chose to call her 'little spells' appeared to be a thing of the past. The household furniture, the crockery, the ornaments were safe. The fit she flung over the college incident was the last.

"I suspected, then knew almost for a certainty the reason for her withdrawal. But it was something I couldn't talk about, either to Cee or Athena —although I tried to feel Athena out, to see how much she had guessed, and finally I decided she was as lacking in sensitivity as she was in humor.

"'What do you mean, have I noticed a change in Celinda?' she asked. 'Of course. She's growing up, finally, and acting more like a lady.'

"'That isn't what I meant,' I said. 'She's so quiet now, Athena. She's just not with us any more.'

"'She talks almost as much as she ever did.'

"'But never about anything that's close to her, only about inconsequential things.' Athena, I decided then, spent too much time with the mechanics of living to know much about life. She not only didn't see the forest, but very few of the trees. I tried again. 'Athena, do you think Cee worries about Uncle Darius?'

" 'For heaven's sake why should she? They've been getting along just fine lately.'

" 'I mean does his preoccupation with her bother her?'

" 'I don't know what you're talking about,' she said. 'He isn't any more preoccupied with Celinda than he is with us—well, not much more. After all, she is the baby and as he said, she's always had a high point of emotionalism. I guess that means she's high-strung.' Athena looked up from her sewing then and said, 'I wouldn't have thought it of you, Beryl, but I do believe you're jealous of your own sister.'

"I was so disgusted at the thought of being jealous of Cee that I left the room. But one thought stayed in my mind. I kept wondering to what extent *Cee* was aware of Uncle Darius' preoccupation with her. Certainly she *was* aware of it, since she was more sensitive to all levels of feeling than the rest of the family, but was this the cause of her 'going off somewhere so nobody could find her?'

"And what of Uncle Darius himself? I wondered about that, too. If he had noticed the change in Celinda, he never mentioned it. He seemed wholly satisfied with everything about his favorite niece. When she was in the room with him, he never took his eyes off her face. He always nodded approvingly whenever she spoke, and I always thought that if God could have meant half as much to him as Celinda did, he would have been a religious fanatic.

"But in a way I could understand his adoration. I think as a child Uncle Darius lived in his twin's shadow. Our father, Donald, was the one with the magnetic personality, the ability to bargain with the world on its own terms and come out ahead. And he was the one with the wife and family. I think Uncle Darius never quite learned how to be anyone other than Donald Quincannon's twin brother. He had probably tried to bargain with loneliness on its terms and been overwhelmingly defeated. And when fate suddenly decreed that he should, in effect, become Donald and take on his responsibilities, Darius Quincannon was unprepared, and therefore unresponding. He had never learned how to love.

"But Celinda sort of sneaked up on him.

"There was little difference in the way he treated the three of us until Celinda was about eight years old. Then, apparently, he became aware of her as a person in her own right and not merely one of his charges. When she spoke she had his full attention, and when she laughed he chuckled with her even when he wasn't sure what was funny, and when she walked across a room he watched her. Somewhere in some corner of his soul, I think he had stored his feelings, unused and forgotten. And Cee brought—"

Beryl stopped suddenly, an awareness not only of Patrick, but of some danger showing in her eyes. Patrick followed her glance toward the slowly opening door and cringed as he saw Athena there, an expression of complete horror on her face.

"Beryl Quincannon, what are you telling him?" she asked. "What in heaven's name are you telling that child?"

# 15

Patrick awoke early the next morning—even before the sun was up—and felt such a great heaviness of body and being that his first conscious thought was to wonder what terrible thing had happened to him the day before. It did not take him long to remember.

Beryl had been interrupted by Athena when she was telling him about Celinda. Now he probably would never know the rest of the story, because he was sure he would never find Beryl in that talkative a mood again.

Just to make himself feel better, he kicked at the wastepaper basket beside his bed as he got up and muttered, "Damn, damn, double damn," but it didn't help, and the basket rolled over with a clatter which was sure to awaken the whole, entire household. "Hell, hell, triple hell," he tried, but found there was not much consolation in hell either. There was one more word he wanted desperately to say, but he didn't dare as long as he was under the same roof with Athena. He had tried the word out on Rusty once, and Rusty had been plenty impressed, but later when Rusty reported what had happened when *he* tried the word out at home, Patrick decided to wait a while before educating his own family—a long while.

He listened at the door for a minute, but heard no sound to indicate that anyone else was awake, although it was about time for Uncle Darius to start brewing the coffee. He dressed and went downstairs, not having the faintest idea where he was going, knowing only that he wanted to get out of the house.

He went out to the front porch, where it was much cooler than the closed, summer-musty-smelling downstairs. Then, for no good reason, he went under the porch, the place where he was supposed to have been asleep the night he had spied on Beryl.

Beryl. How in the living hell would he *ever* get her to finish the story about Celinda? Athena had all but scared him spitless when she appeared like a specter in the doorway, so he could imagine how Beryl felt, caught telling something she was never supposed to tell while the world stood. However, after first jumping out of her skin, Beryl had seemed calm enough.

"Patrick couldn't sleep. It's so hot in his room," she'd said. "So I invited him to come in here until it cools off a bit. I was telling him a bedtime story."

"Humph!" Athena said, sounding for all the world like Uncle Darius. "If you ask me, he's too old for bedtime stories. And he's entirely too old to be spoiled the way you spoil him, Beryl."

Beryl didn't say anything, just smiled a sort of small, sad smile, then whopped Patrick over the backside and said, "Off to bed now, buster."

"But Beryl, you didn't finish . . ."

"Enough for tonight," she said quickly. "I'm sleepy, even if you aren't."

"Will you finish the story tomorrow?" He had to have her promise.

"I don't know," she said, looking at Athena who still hovered in the door, looking very much like a buzzard just waiting for them to stop moving before devouring them. "I don't know."

It was no use, Patrick knew. Athena, the buzzard, had spoiled everything.

He heard a board squeak overhead, somewhere on the first floor of the house, and knew that Uncle Darius had come down to get the coffee going. He'd bet that if the temperature went to 164 degrees Fahrenheit—and it seemed fairly close to that now—Uncle Darius still would have to start the day with hot coffee. The area under the porch probably was the coolest place in Laurelton, except for the places that had air-conditioning. One thing for sure, he knew, the Quincannons would never have air-conditioning, because Uncle Darius thought it was unhealthy.

"It goes against nature," he said. "It is supposed to be hot in the summer and cold in the winter. That's the way the good Lord intended it, and that's the way it is going to be in this household."

"I'm surprised we have heat in the winter," Beryl said, and Patrick had expected Uncle Darius to light into her with a sermon, but he had only given her one of those frowns which made his face look as though it had been plowed up.

Patrick decided he would spend most of the day under the porch. At one end enough light came through so he could see to read, and he liked the cool, earthy smell. Besides, he just plain didn't feel like socializing with Athena and Uncle Darius all day.

More boards squeaked overhead, and he knew that Mavis had come in to cook breakfast. When he went up to breakfast he would get his book, ask Mavis to fix him some sandwiches for a picnic lunch, and then he'd come back under the porch and spend the whole, entire day.

The plan worked well during the morning. Of course he had to help Uncle Darius with his paste-ups first, but he did that while Mavis was making the sandwiches for him.

"Would you mind fixing me a thermos of lemonade, too?" he asked.

"Where you going, Patrick?" she asked. "You and that Rusty up to some kind of devilment?"

"Of course not, Mavis." He decided not to explain anything. He was worn out with everybody knowing everything about him anyway, especially when he, apparently, was not to be given the knowledge he wanted about others.

It was during the early afternoon that he began to weary of his retirement. He had finished the book, the lunch was long since eaten, and he was about to crawl out and check on what Rusty was doing when the board directly over his head groaned beneath a weight that was certainly not Athena's. Besides, Athena probably was watching a soap opera, and it was Uncle Darius' after-lunch nap time. Nobody ever came calling at this hour. In fact, nobody came calling, period. At least, not often. Only those who didn't know better—like Father Conroy, and he certainly wouldn't be back any time soon.

He heard the doorbell ringing in the house and then heard Athena say, "Why, Louis, this is a surprise."

"Hello, Athena, how're you doing? Is Mr. Quincannon home?"

Great day in the morning! Patrick thought, hardly breathing. It was Louis Nichols, and there wasn't but one thing that Patrick could think of that would bring him calling on Uncle Darius during the day while Beryl was at the shop. He had come to tell Uncle Darius all about Beryl and Christopher Danton.

"Won't you come in?" Athena said. "He's in the library. I'll call him."

"I hate to disturb him," Louis said, "but it is rather important that I talk to him now. I'll just wait out here. There's a nice breeze and these chairs look inviting."

Patrick crawled nearer to the center of the house so he could hear better. It seemed quite a while before he heard the screen door slam and Uncle Darius saying without greeting or preamble, "Well, Louis, what can I do for you?"

"Good afternoon, Mr. Quincannon. How are you, sir?"

"My health does well enough for a man of my years. Is that what you came here at this hour of the day to find out?"

Louis coughed. "No, sir, not exactly."

"I thought as much." Uncle Darius apparently had sat down in the only rocker on the porch, because the two boards just above Patrick's head began a steady, rhythmic squeaking. That meant

Louis had to be sitting either in the swing (and obviously he hadn't because the chains on that squeaked audibly also) or on one of the hard wrought-iron chairs, and the poor man was surely uncomfortable in more ways than one.

"I'll tell you why you're here," Uncle Darius said, "and save you the trouble of having to tell me. You're here to represent that Yankee fellow, that what's-his-name, who has decided maybe you can get further with me than he can. Well, Louis, you can just go straight back to him and tell him my original answer stands. Not one fraction of an acre of Quincannon land will be sold while there's breath in my body."

"Excuse me, Mr. Quincannon, but you've got it all wrong," Louis said. "I work for Danton Fabrics, but I didn't come here for Christopher Danton. In fact, he doesn't know I'm here."

Jumping Judas! here it comes now, Patrick thought. Louis was getting ready to let so many skeletons out of Beryl's closet that the Quincannon yard would look like a family reunion in Spooksville.

Uncle Darius' voice sounded a bit friendlier as he said, "Then I beg your pardon, Louis, if I have misjudged your motives. I never could understand why you allied yourself . . ."

"I'm here representing the people of Laurelton, Mr. Quincannon," Louis interrupted. "I'm sure you are aware of the fact that almost every town in the South, big and little, has an industrial committee which courts northern industry. The committee does everything in its power—and the power of the town and county—to get new industry.

"Laurelton is no exception, as you know. Our industrial committee has worked very hard and has done an excellent job, particularly in the past few years. This town found out eleven years ago when the paper plant moved here what could be done with more money—a better economy. The biggest coup of all, of course, was getting Danton Fabrics here. The payroll of that one business alone assures us that Laurelton will never wither and die on the vine the way so many small towns have in the South. We can't depend on agriculture any more, sir. Haven't been able to for years. It's more than just a matter of *wanting* industry, we've *got to have it*."

It was probably one of the hottest days this side of August, but Patrick could imagine icicles forming around Uncle Darius' next words.

"So you're not representing that Yankee fellow."

"I've come to see you on behalf of the people of Laurelton and Laurel County," Louis said. "To be perfectly frank, it was Maurice Maynard who suggested that I have a talk with you. He's chairman of the industrial committee, you know."

"Speak your piece then, so you can tell him you did. And the answer you can take back to him is the same one I quoted to you earlier."

"I don't believe you fully understand the seriousness of this, Mr. Quincannon. This is the only property available—"

"That's your mistake, Louis. It isn't available."

"I mean it's the only property in the business

section of Laurelton that has enough land for the type of building that Danton Fabrics wants to erect. And Christopher Danton has let it be known within the past two days that unless they get this property, the plant will be moved to Macontown, two hundred miles away."

"And you believed him? I wouldn't have expected naïveté from you, Louis. The plant has been in operation here for almost a year. They certainly won't pull out now."

"It's in operation in a rented building just outside the city limits. And it wouldn't be difficult at this stage to move the whole shebang," Louis said. "The Macontown industrial committee has promised not only a new building for the plant, rent-free for the first five years with option to buy after that, but also space in the center of town for an office building."

"Would you mind telling me why this particular factory can't have offices in the plant itself, like any other normal factory?" Uncle Darius' words sounded like daggers aimed straight for Louis.

"I thought you knew, sir," Louis said. "They plan to make this the home office for all the Danton plants. When Mr. Danton Senior died—that was about the time Danton Fabrics came here—the four sons decided to make some sweeping changes. Moving the home office from New Jersey is one of the changes."

There was a long silence, then Louis said, "So you can see, Mr. Quincannon, everything depends on you. You might say the future of all of Laurel County depends on you."

"*You* might say it, I wouldn't," Uncle Darius said. "You seem to be forgetting that it was a Quincannon who first settled in this county. Quincannons have served as mayors, town commissioners, school board chairmen—you name any board, any civic project you want to and you'll find a Quincannon was very much involved in the well-being of this county. So don't come to me, Louis Nichols, and talk about the future of the county. If it hadn't been for the Quincannons, the county wouldn't even have had a past, let alone a present or future."

"But, sir—"

"And I don't care if the governor of the state himself wants to put his office where my home is, the answer is still NO! Good day to you, Louis."

The rocker stopped squeaking, the screen door slammed. Patrick crawled out from the porch just in time to see Louis go through the front gate. He looked toward the porch, deserted now.

There was no question about it, no question at all. This was the biggest mess in the whole, entire world. Laurelton was going to lose its biggest business, the Quincannon family was going to lose all its friends, Beryl was going to lose her boy friend, and he, Patrick, was going to end up the biggest loser of all, because if Beryl found out she was going to spend the rest of her life in that house with Uncle Darius and Athena, she'd never, ever tell him anything else about Celinda. She'd be too afraid of the consequences of breaking her promise to Uncle Darius.

He would lose his mother, just when he had

found her. Just when he was beginning to know her.

There would never be a better time than right this very minute to say that word, he decided, and he didn't care much if Athena heard him. He glared at the front door, almost willing her to come and listen as he said, "Great mountainous mounds of shining *shit!*"

Patrick slipped in the front door and stood in the hall by the brass umbrella stand, listening. He was sure he would hear Uncle Darius sounding off to Athena about Louis Nichols joining "that Yankee fellow" in trying to turn the Quincannon family out of their home. But the house was as quiet as if the family already had moved.

That would never happen, Patrick knew for sure, as long as there was breath in Uncle Darius' body.

He went through the kitchen to the back porch, and just as he started outside he glimpsed Uncle Darius walking rapidly through the clearing to the woods. That meant only one thing: Uncle Darius was too upset even to talk to Athena. He never went to the woods unless he had something on his mind, something serious. But probably by the time he came out of the woods, he would be ready to let fly with an oration that would turn into a sermon, and the congregation would, of course, consist of Athena, Beryl, and Patrick—at dinner, most likely.

There had to be a way he could stop Uncle Darius from telling Beryl that Christopher Danton was going to move Danton Fabrics out of Laurelton. At least, he had to keep her from knowing it until he had a chance to hear the rest of the Celinda story. But how?

He sat down on the steps in his favorite thinking position, chin cupped in hands. Maybe if Uncle Darius blew off steam to him and Athena before Beryl got home, it would tone down or even prevent a later eruption. But even if he were comparatively calm by then, he'd still tell Beryl the news and maybe even brag because he was the one who was getting rid of what he had been calling "Laurelton's latest unwanted element."

It all looked hopeless—for everybody. Several times in his life he had wished that Natalie and Louis Nichols would adopt him so Rusty could have a brother. He thought of that now. That would be one way of having a family like everyone else's. . . . Another thought ruined the first one. There was another loser that he had forgotten when he was making up his list of losers. Louis Nichols would lose his job when the plant moved, or if he kept the job, he and his family would move to Macontown. Either way, Rusty would no longer be his friend, and it was reasonable to assume that the Nichols family would not be speaking to any of the Quincannons, even the one whose last name happened to be Tolson.

For one wild minute he thought of running into the woods and calling, "Uncle Darius, sell the property! It's all right if we have to live somewhere else, because nothing is ever going to be the same again anyway, not even if we keep living here."

He remained where he was, knowing perfectly well that Uncle Darius never changed his mind about anything.

He sat on the steps for a long, long time and came no closer to a solution. Finally, he began to wonder why Uncle Darius was spending so much time in the woods. He had never to Patrick's knowledge stayed this long before.

He got up and walked to the edge of the clearing, peering through the trees and listening. The woods were as still as the house. Even the breeze which had rustled the leaves earlier, making the sound of flowing water, had stopped. It was as still as . . . death. That thought which had sneaked up on him unawares held him in terror.

Should he go to tell Athena that Uncle Darius might have died in the woods? Might at this very minute be lying dead as a doornail beside the white marble tombstone?

He took a few cautious steps through the beginning of the thicket, then a few more. Perhaps he'd better not tell Athena anything until he knew for sure.

It was broad daylight, but the woods had never looked spookier. He had not felt that frightened even the night he dug up the grave. Then he had half expected to find a skeleton, and now. . . .

He tried not to think about what he would find

as he made his way slowly and quietly toward the small clearing where the tombstone was.

The marble gleamed brightly in the sun rays that came through the tree limbs. Patrick was almost in the clearing before he saw Uncle Darius. The reason he had not spotted him immediately was that Uncle Darius—dignified, unbending Uncle Darius—was sitting on the ground beside the tombstone.

He wasn't doing one earthly thing that Patrick could see except moving his right hand over the marble, slowly tracing with his finger the words *Requiescat in Pace.*

"What in tarnation . . ." Patrick clamped his hand over his mouth. The words had slipped out. He waited, expecting Uncle Darius to jump to his feet and start preaching a sermon right then and there to cover his embarrassment at being found doing something so dumb-stupid. But Uncle Darius apparently had not heard. He stopped tracing the words, but he leaned against the tombstone, his head resting against the name "Celinda." His eyes closed and he breathed deeply.

Asleep, Patrick thought. If that doesn't just hare-lip the governor! Uncle Darius sitting on the ground, leaning against a tombstone, sound asleep, and it was almost time for him to go to the shop to walk home with Beryl.

Patrick caught his breath. That was it! He crept away from the clearing, then ran through the woods as fast as he could. If Uncle Darius just wouldn't wake up for a while, he could get to Beryl first and maybe hear the rest of the story before Uncle Darius fixed it so she'd never tell him.

He did not stop running when he reached the house, but went flying through the yard, out the gate, and down the street toward the shop where Beryl worked. She was just coming out when he reached the door.

"Patrick, my goodness, what's your hurry?" she asked. "Has something happened?"

"No," he panted. "Uncle Darius wasn't around to meet you," he had to stop to take a breath, "so I decided to."

"That's nice," Beryl said. "Where's Uncle Darius?"

"Oh, he's probably around somewhere," Patrick said, and then, quickly, as they started walking, "Beryl, will you tell me the rest of it now?"

"The rest of it?"

"About Celinda."

"There's too much to tell and it's too hot for strolling."

"When we get home then? Please. We can go to your room. Please, Beryl."

"I suppose . . . unless there's something Athena wants me to do."

Athena apparently was in the kitchen with Mavis when they arrived, and they went to Beryl's room unobserved. Beryl closed the door and said, "If you're going to sit on the bed, take off your shoes, Patrick. That spread has just been cleaned." Then, as he made himself comfortable, "I don't know about telling you any more."

"You have to, Beryl. You promised!" he burst out.

"No, I haven't promised you anything. On the other hand, I have promised Uncle Darius. . . ."

He tried to appeal to her reason. "I'll find out sooner or later from somebody, so isn't it better for you to tell me?" The truth was, and he knew it, he might never find out from anybody. "Last night you stopped where Celinda had 'gone away somewhere so nobody could find her,' and that was before she really went away, you said."

Beryl sat in the little rocker across from him and was quiet for a while. Then her eyes began to get the same dreamy, faraway look they had had last night. Finally, she started talking. "I don't know which happened to Cee first, the Catholic Church or Jason Tolson. I rather think it was at church that she met Jason, but nobody could ever convince Uncle Darius of this. He always believed it was Jason who lured Celinda into his church. And anything that took her out of his sight, particularly if it used up any of her love and loyalty, became immediately a demoralizing influence. So he looked upon Jason as corrupt and the church as corrupting.

"Cee and I weren't very close during this time. I had begun to get bored with staying home all day, so I started working in the dress shop, never dreaming I'd make it a lifetime career.

"Cee's restlessness after she finished high school was noticed finally even by Athena. One day she said to me, 'I wish I could count the times Celinda has been in and out of the house today. In and out of that car all day. I wonder where she goes.'

"I made no comment because at the moment I wasn't too interested, and also because I thought Cee's comings and goings were her own business.

It was too much, the way everybody tried to keep track of her all the time as though she were a mentally incompetent infant!

"There were other comments from Athena during that summer, a great many comments from Mavis, and even a few from Uncle Darius. Comments like, 'Celinda is running herself ragged and I don't even know doing what. If you ask her anything, all you get is an evasive answer.'

"There was a feeling of uneasiness among us all that summer, and I think we were all aware of it. Cee continued to stay away for hours at a time, and where she went remained her secret. I imagined her speeding recklessly down country roads, releasing tension that way.

"But sometime in the fall, about October I think, we noticed a change in Celinda. The restlessness was gone. She was no longer a discontent gadfly, but was quiet and had a new serenity that was almost startling after the other extreme of her nature.

"Mavis was the first to remark on it. 'She's settling down now. Don't you worry no more about Miss Cee, she'll be all right. I feel it in my bones.'

"And Athena said, 'I hope it isn't just the cool weather that's slowed her down. I'd hate to think what would happen if we had an Indian summer.'

"Several times I started to ask Cee if something had happened to change her, but I never did. I decided if she wanted to confide in me, she would. At any rate, everyone, especially Uncle Darius, was happier with the new Celinda. For one thing, she stayed home more, going out only occasionally during the day and then usually to the library, because she had become an avid reader. She brought home books of philosophy, history, religion, poetry, everything you can imagine.

"She also dated less often, and most of the time she was in the house even before Uncle Darius' ten o'clock curfew. You know, I always wondered why a curfew was imposed upon Celinda when Athena and I had never been told any special time to be in. Either Uncle Darius trusted us and wasn't sure about Cee, or else it didn't matter to him what time we came in, but it mattered greatly with Cee.

"It was in December that I got the biggest surprise yet where Cee was concerned. And it answered some of my questions as to where she had been during those many hours she was not at home in the summer.

"She asked me one night, 'Berry, could you get away from the shop for a little while tomorrow?'

"'Get away? Why? This is the rush season, with Christmas almost here.'

"'I know, but I thought for just a little while. . . .' Her forehead puckered into a frown and then she said, 'Please, it won't take long.'

"'Maybe I can arrange it, but what for?'

"'I'm being baptized tomorrow, and I want you and Mavis to go with me. Uncle Darius and Athena don't know about it, and I'd rather they didn't right now.'

"'*Baptized!* What on earth are you talking about? You were christened when you were a baby.'

" 'This is different. I'm becoming a Catholic to-morrow. I've been taking instruction in the church for several months and—'

" 'A Catholic! Cee, you're joking. You're a Methodist. Why'd you take instruction in another church?'

" 'I don't know, really. It just sort of happened.' The expression on her face was beautiful. 'During the summer I went with Mary Flannagan to Mass one Sunday and—I don't know—I can't describe how I felt. After that, I started going to St. Anne's alone, in the afternoons when no one was there and . . . Well, as I said I can't describe it to you, and I doubt if you would understand it even if I could. Then one day I met Father Conroy outside the church and started talking to him, and he offered to give me instruction. . . . Well, that's it. This is something I want more than I've ever wanted anything. I didn't dare say a word to anybody, because I knew Uncle Darius would forbid it. He's always against everything I've ever really wanted. So—tomorrow I'm being baptized, and I want you and Mavis there. And I want you not to say anything to Uncle Darius and Athena.'

"My first impulse was to say, 'Cee, you've completely flipped,' but just looking at her stopped me. All I said was, 'Okay, I'll be there. What time?'

Patrick chortled. "I'll bet Uncle Darius was the one who flipped when he found out. I think he hates Catholics even worse than he does Yankees."

"He didn't completely blow a fuse when he found out," Beryl said. "I expected him to, but he didn't. He found out the following Sunday morning

when Cee left the house, announcing that she was
going to Mass. She added nonchalantly, 'I'm a member of St. Anne's now, you know. I joined the
church last week.'

"I'm really not sure what Uncle Darius thought.
He said very little, probably because it was too
late to stop Cee. And he didn't have the feeling
against the church then that he does now. He
thought everything Cee did was perfect, and if
she wanted the Catholic Church, I'm sure he was
sorry he could not present it to her as a gift,
along with the Vatican, the Pope, and the College
of Cardinals.

"His feeling against the church, if he had any,
didn't show until right before Christmas, when we
first met Jason Tolson and Uncle Darius found
out he was a Catholic. He decided immediately
that Jaybird had talked Cee into joining his church.

"No one knew exactly when Cee had begun
seeing Jaybird, or, for that matter, when he had
come to Laurelton to live. The family met him for
the first time when he called at the house for Cee,
and it was obvious that he and Cee had known
each other for some time."

"What did you think of him when you first
met him?" Patrick asked immediately.

"The first thing about Jason Tolson that struck
me was his indifference, not only toward Celinda's
family, but toward Cee herself. And no one had
ever been indifferent toward her before. Athena
met Jaybird at the door and showed him into the
living room while Cee was still upstairs dressing.
Uncle Darius stood up immediately and had the expression of a king inspecting the royal guard. Be-

fore Athena could introduce him, Uncle Darius stuck out his hand. 'How do you do, sir? I suppose you're here to see Celinda. I'm Darius Quincannon, her uncle.'

"'How do you do?' Jason Tolson said, as though he couldn't care less."

"What did he look like?" Patrick asked.

"He was rather handsome, but in an average way," Beryl said, a slight frown on her face as though she didn't like to picture him in her mind, let alone talk about him. "He had brown hair which waved just above his forehead. This gave him a boyish look, but there was nothing boyish about his eyes—steel gray and just as hard. He had an evaluating look he gave everything that made me cringe. And, most surprising of all, he was at least ten years older than Celinda—certainly much older than anyone she had ever dated before.

"'I don't believe I caught your name,' Uncle Darius said.

"'Tolson.'

"'Tolson, Tolson,' Uncle Darius repeated. 'I don't believe I know any Tolsons around here.'

"'I'm not from around here,' he said. 'I'm from Connecticut originally.'

"'When you say originally, I gather you no longer call Connecticut home.'

"'No, I call Laurelton home now.' He looked completely bored with the inquisition.

"'What line of work are you in?'

"'I'm a management consultant.'

"'You must be here with that new paper factory that moved down from the North.'

"'That's right.'

"'How long have you been in Laurelton? I don't recall having seen you before—not even at church. I take it you're not a Methodist. Baptist, maybe?'

"'I'm a Roman Catholic.'

"'A Rom—' Uncle Darius stopped as though his tongue were suddenly paralyzed, and I could hear his thoughts as clearly as if they were being played back to me on a tape recorder.

"A Roman Catholic. Dating Celinda, who had just turned Catholic without having given any reason at all for doing so. Now the reason was perfectly clear. Jason Tolson. And that meant Celinda must be serious about Jason Tolson.

"I knew in that instant that Uncle Darius not only hated Jason Tolson, but his church as well, and even the business that had brought him to Laurelton.

"Celinda came in then, looking positively radiant, the most beautiful thing I've ever seen. But when Jason looked at her there was no real appreciation in his eyes that I could see. Only the same indifference that he had registered ever since entering the house. They were hardly out the door before Uncle Darius began pacing the living room. He had forgotten to remind Cee about the curfew. For a while he didn't say anything, then he stopped in the middle of the floor and raised his arms and shouted, 'How long has Celinda been seeing that man? Do either of you know?'

"Neither Athena nor I had the slightest idea, of course.

"'She is never to see him again,' Uncle Darius said. 'I'll see to that.'

" 'If you forbid her to see him, you'll only make her more interested—if she *is* interested, that is,' Athena said.

" 'Hummmph!' Uncle Darius raised his arms again as though about to deliver a sermon worthy of Cotton Mather, then lowered his arms, turned, and left the room. We could hear him for hours after that, pacing in the library.

"It was after eleven when she got home, and the only reason Uncle Darius did not meet her at the door and send Jason Tolson away was that he was so busy with his pacing and thinking that he didn't hear Celinda come in. And then, too, I don't think he expected her that early. She went to her room without seeing him.

"The next morning at breakfast, Uncle Darius' first words to her were, 'You are not to go out with a young man again for a month, and you are never to see that Tolson man again under any circumstances.'

"I held my breath, waiting for the dishes to start flying, but nothing happened. Cee looked at Uncle Darius, smiled slightly, and began to eat her breakfast."

"Uncle Darius couldn't do a thing with Celinda, could he?" Patrick asked delightedly. "How long before she saw Jason again?"

Beryl closed her eyes. "The next day. Christmas. It was just like any other Christmas until that night. Cee was rather quiet during the day, but we had come to expect that of her. She had gone to the midnight Mass at St. Anne's the night before. Come to think of it, I suppose she saw Jason then. Anyway, there was nothing Uncle Darius could do about that. We had our Christmas dinner in the middle of the day, and late in the afternoon Cee announced she was going to go for a ride 'to get some air.' I almost said, 'I'll go with you,' but something about the way she looked made me think she might want to be alone.

"Athena made turkey sandwiches for supper and then put a damp cloth over them so they would be fresh when Celinda returned, but when she wasn't back by seven, the rest of us ate our supper.

" 'If she's meeting that Tolson man, I won't allow her out of the house for a month,' Uncle Darius said.

"I reminded him that she had said she was just going to ride.

" 'Maybe she's had car trouble,' Athena said.

"I remember thinking later it was strange that Uncle Darius seemed to know instinctively where Cee was, and Athena and I never guessed.

"At nine o'clock Athena said, 'I think we should call the police or the sheriff's office and have them check some of the roads around here. I'm sure something has happened to Cee, or she would have been back by now.'

" 'We will not call any law enforcement group,' Uncle Darius said. 'I won't have this family touched by scandal.'

" 'An accident is hardly scandalous,' Athena said.

" 'You will respect my wishes in this,' Uncle Darius said, putting an end to the discussion.

"A little later I went upstairs, deciding that Cee was being flagrantly disobedient. I thought she had gone with Jason Tolson to a Christmas party.

When I turned on the light in my room, I saw the note propped up on the dresser. I'll never forget that note. Or the way I felt when I read it—as though I had been kicked in the stomach.

"'Berry dear, I have gone away, and I do hope my departure will not upset your Christmas too much. I am very happy and I want the rest of you to be happy, too, you especially. Jason and I are going to be married. We will not be returning to Laurelton, because his work is finished here. I'll write you as soon as we're situated. Merry Christmas, Berry, and love to you and Athena and Uncle Darius. Cee.'

"I read the note several times before I really understood. Then I took it downstairs and showed it to Athena. 'I don't believe it,' she said, looking as if someone had delivered her a personal insult. Finally, she started toward the library where Uncle Darius was.

"'Don't show it to him,' I whispered. 'Not yet, anyway. Let's wait until morning in case Cee changes her mind and comes back.'

"'I don't think she has a mind to change,' Athena said, 'and anyway Uncle Darius is planning to sit up until she comes in.'

"Uncle Darius was sitting in his big chair with the newspaper spread across his knees when Athena gave him the note. It took him a long time to read it, and when he finally looked up I was shocked at the expression on his face. There was no surprise, no anger, not even grief, only a terrible blankness, a kind of vacant stare that made me wonder if in that one minute his mind had gone completely.

His hand moved slowly as he crumpled the note and threw it into the fireplace. He watched it burn, then got to his feet with such an effort that I wanted to help him, but for some reason, I was afraid to go nearer to him. He was like a man too old and too feeble to care for his own needs. He walked out of the room, unconsciously reaching out to furniture on the way to keep from falling. He went to the kitchen, poured a glass of water, forgot to drink it, then went back to the library.

"Athena and I had been following him, wondering what to do, and we stopped in the living room to talk it over. We decided there was nothing we *could* do except call in the police to look for Cee, maybe get the highway patrol to stop them before they got to the state line. But then Uncle Darius had said he didn't want that, so we did nothing. Athena finally went to her room, and I went to the library to see if there was anything, anything at all, I could do for Uncle Darius.

"He was sitting at his desk, staring straight ahead and making a strange choking sound, as though he might be strangling. When I got nearer, I saw he was crying. He didn't put his head down or even cover his eyes. He sat bolt upright at the desk with tears pouring from his eyes like twin streams and his shoulders heaving as he made that terrible rasping noise in his throat.

"I was so terrified, I ran out of the room."

"What happened then?" Patrick asked.

Beryl shuddered as though she were actually reliving the days which followed Celinda's departure. "None of us ever had much to say about Cee's elopement, not even to each other," she said. "I guess the hurt went too deep for discussion. Or maybe Mavis said all there was to say the next day when she learned what had happened. She threw her apron over her face and broke down, saying, 'Oh, my sweet baby! Why'd she want to go and do a thing like that? Why'd she want to run away with that Jaybird who don't love her half as much as we do? Jesus God!'

"It was only a day or two after that that Uncle Darius, in control of himself once more, gave the orders. 'You are not to mention that man's name in this house, and you are to mention Celinda's name only when it is absolutely necessary. And if you will stop to think before speaking, I believe you'll find that it can, most times, be avoided. You are to throw away any pictures you have of Celinda, whether large pictures or snapshots. I demand this of all of you,' his glance included Mavis, too, 'and to disobey me will go hard with you. You,' this time he looked at me, 'are to clean out her room of all personal effects. If she left any clothes, take them to the Salvation Army. Everything else is to be thrown away or burned. And I don't want you, in a moment of weak sentimentality, to save anything. Not *anything*.'

"Athena gasped. 'You're acting as though she's dead.'

"'No, not dead, Athena. For us she never existed.' He went to the front of the house and looked out the window at the empty driveway where not too long before the red convertible had crunched over the gravel when Celinda had gone to 'get some air.' I wanted to go to him and say, 'Don't do these things and don't make us do them. Cee might decide she made a mistake. She might get homesick and want to come back.' But I didn't because I knew Cee would not come back, and it would have been a terrible thing to get Uncle Darius' hopes up, as well as my own.

"In the spring he had the driveway in front of the house plowed up and grass seed sowed where the driveway had been. He had the iron gate, matching the fence, put at the end of the drive, and by summer, when the grass came up, you could not tell there had ever been a driveway in front of the Quincannon house."

# 17

"Beryl, are you up there?" Athena's voice from downstairs.

Beryl opened the door and called, "Yes, Athena, I'm home. And Patrick's with me, in case you're looking for him."

"I was, as a matter of fact. Supper's in five minutes."

Damn, damn, double damn, Patrick thought. Now Beryl would go downstairs, hear the news from Uncle Darius, and that would be that. Why couldn't supper have been late just this once?

"Better go wash up now, Patrick," Beryl said.

"You know how Uncle Darius is if he's kept waiting at the table. Athena, too."

"Beryl, will you promise me something?" Patrick
said solemnly. "Will you cross-your-heart-and-
hope-to-die, then-you'll-eat-a-dead-pig's-eye if you
don't tell me the rest of the story?"

"Sometime, Patrick. Obviously we can't talk any
more right now."

"After supper then?"

"We'll see."

This was not enough for Patrick. He knew that
with Natalie Nichols "we'll see" meant yes. With
Athena it meant "I don't want to hear any more
about it." With Mavis it meant "Yes, but stop
bothering me right this minute." With Beryl it
meant exactly "We'll see." Maybe yes, maybe no.

Athena and Uncle Darius already were in the
dining room when he and Beryl went downstairs.
He studied Uncle Darius' face, trying to figure
out what kind of mood he was in—a preaching
one, a mad one, or just an ordinary Uncle Darius
one, which sort of took in everything.

"Beryl," Uncle Darius said immediately, "I am
sorry I was not available to walk you home this
afternoon. The truth is, something quite serious
came up, and it completely slipped my mind until
past time for you to have been home."

Beryl gave Uncle Darius a funny look, and
Patrick knew she was wondering what could have
been serious enough to keep him from his daily
walk with her. Usually only illness prevented it.

"It's all right, Uncle Darius," she said. "Patrick
escorted me home. He took your place and met me
at the door of the shop just as I was coming out."

Uncle Darius nodded, sat for a minute in silence, and then, as though that, also, had almost slipped his mind, he asked the blessing.

It began as one of the quietest meals Patrick could remember, because nobody said anything until just before Mavis brought in the dessert. The amount of conversation usually depended upon whether Uncle Darius was in a talkative mood or not, and tonight he was in about the most untalkative mood Patrick had ever seen.

This suited him just fine. If Uncle Darius would wait until tomorrow to tell Beryl what had happened—or rather, what was going to happen—there might be a chance of getting Beryl to finish the story tonight.

It was Athena who ruined everything.

"You haven't told Beryl about your visitor this afternoon," she said to Uncle Darius.

Uncle Darius sighed extravagantly, as though he were the most put-upon person in the whole, entire world. "Louis Nichols came to see me this afternoon, Beryl."

"Athena, may I have some more mashed potatoes, please," Patrick said loudly.

It didn't work. Athena reached out silently for his plate while Uncle Darius went on talking.

"I had thought better of Louis all these years," he said.

"Better than what?" Beryl asked. "What did he want?"

"He wanted me to sell this property to his boss, of course. What else would he want? He's turned out to be a traitor to everything his family ever stood for. Just give a man a little more money than he's used to, a little more prestige and a few people to boss around, and he goes power-mad. I never thought it of Louis, but that's exactly what happened."

"Perhaps you misunderstood his motives, Uncle Darius," Beryl said. "I've heard Louis say several times that if you held out long enough, you could get Danton Fabrics to go up even more on their offer. I suppose now he thinks they've gone as high as they'll go, and so he was advising you to sell."

"Hummph! He was thinking about himself and nothing more," Uncle Darius said. "What's happened is that Macontown is trying to lure the industry there, and that Danton man has decided that if he can't have this very site for an office building, he's going to move, lock, stock, and barrel, to Macontown."

"Move Danton Fabrics—everything?" Beryl suddenly turned the color of the white table cloth.

"That's what Louis said, but I don't believe him," Uncle Darius said. "I've spent a long time thinking about it, and I think Louis was just trying to use any tactic he could think of to make me sell. I'm sure that Yankee fellow put him up to it, but I never thought I'd see the day Louis could be so easily corrupted."

"If Louis said the plant is moving, it's true," Beryl whispered. "He wouldn't lie." She began coughing as though she was going into a paroxysm, and although the cough didn't sound entirely legitimate to Patrick, Beryl excused herself and fled from the table. They heard her running up-stairs.

"Swallowed something the wrong way, I suppose," Athena said. After a few minutes, when Beryl did not return, Athena went to the foot of the stairs and called, "Aren't you going to come back for dessert, Beryl?"

"No, I don't have time," Beryl answered. "I'm going over to see Natalie."

Uncle Darius got up and joined Athena at the foot of the stairs. "I'd rather you didn't remain too friendly with those people, Beryl, now that they've showed us what they are."

"I don't think you have to worry about that, Uncle Darius." Beryl came downstairs. "It isn't likely that they'll be very interested in the friendship of any member of the Quincannon family after this."

The screen door slammed as Beryl went out, and Uncle Darius and Athena apparently forgot to come back to the table, because Patrick heard them going into the living room. He sat alone at the table, sticking his spoon disconsolately into the small yellow mound of rice pudding. It was all going exactly as he had known it would. And furthermore, he could predict—had already predicted—everything that would happen from now on. He thought now he knew what it would be like to write a play and then see it acted out, because the play he had composed in his mind this afternoon was being acted out now almost word for word as he had composed it. And it wouldn't change tomorrow either, or the day after that.

He could picture the entire rest of his life, day after endless day, droning on in the pattern he knew by heart already.

He left the rice pudding and went through the kitchen to the back porch. He wanted suddenly to see Rusty. He wanted to see him very much, and he didn't want to have to explain to Athena or Uncle Darius where he was going.

"Y'all finished, Patrick?" Mavis asked before he went out.

"We sure are," he said. "We're finished, all right."

He cut around to the front of the house after he was outside, went through the gate, and walked slowly down the street toward Rusty's. He wished now he had gone when Beryl did. Perhaps they could have cheered each other up a little bit, or maybe have sympathized with each other, since he didn't really think there was any way either of them could ever be cheered up again.

Rusty was sitting on his front porch, in Patrick's thinking position. He didn't move a muscle or say a word as Patrick came down the walk. Taking his cue from this, Patrick said nothing either but sat down beside Rusty.

"Are y'all going or staying?" he asked finally.

"Going or staying where?" Rusty asked.

"Here."

"Patrick, sometimes I think you're just plain nuts. What in tarnation are you talking about?"

"Is your daddy going to move to Macontown with Danton Fabrics, or is he going to stay here and look for another job?" Patrick was patience itself.

Rusty's mouth dropped open. "That's what they're talking about, I'll bet. That's why they chased me away."

"Now what in tarnation are *you* talking about?"

"Mama and Daddy and Beryl and Chris Danton are all sitting out on the back patio talking, and they told me to go play somewhere else. I thought it was because Daddy was going to fix drinks for them and they didn't want me to see them drinking."

"Haven't they told you *any*thing that's going on?" Patrick asked.

"Nothing like what you're talking about," Rusty said. "What about moving to Macontown?"

But Patrick did not want to waste time explaining to Rusty when he might be learning something himself—though what there was left to find out, he couldn't imagine. "Let's sneak back there and listen," he suggested. "You can find out everything that way."

Rusty stood up, as usual agreeable to anything Patrick wanted to do. What an advantage age was, Patrick thought as they went around the house. "Where can we hide?" he asked.

"In the japonica bushes," Rusty said. "We can crawl through them and be practically on the patio."

They dropped to all fours and stopped talking. Patrick felt a sharp scratch on his cheek as he inched his way across the ground under the bushes, but he didn't have time to think about it now. And, unless it left a scar, he probably wouldn't have time to think about it later. He found a place, still under the bushes, right at the edge of the patio, where he could not only hear every word but also could see Beryl and Natalie, who sat facing him. Louis and Danton had their backs to the japonica.

Natalie was crying, he saw that immediately. She wasn't making a sound, or saying anything, but tears were running down her face and she didn't do a thing to stop them. Beryl wasn't crying, but she looked as if she wanted to.

"It isn't just myself, Chris, you know that," Louis was saying. "I'm thinking about all of them. There are over two hundred people working for you who won't be given the choice you've given me. Over two hundred people out of work."

"I see your point, Louis, but they must have been doing *something* before Danton Fabrics came here. I wish you'd all stop trying to make me feel like an utter heel. You know I'm only one vote on the board and I was outvoted. Even my brothers voted against staying here unless—"

"They were doing something," Louis interrupted. "There are two lines in this county that have always been very long, Chris. The line to the unemployment checks and the line to the welfare department. Taking Danton Fabrics away will increase the length of both those lines."

"And perhaps shorten those lines in Macon County. Oh, what the hell!" Danton stood up and began to pace the patio. "You know where I stand, what I think. I'm not going to defend my part in this any longer. I thought I didn't have to with the three people I considered my best friends here. If that old son-of-a-bitch—and if you think I'm going to apologize for calling your uncle that, you're crazy, Beryl, I'd like to call him worse— if that old son-of-a-bitch could think of something besides the goddamn motheaten traditions of his family. Oh, what the hell! He's stark, raving crazy anyway. Only an insane person would put up a tomb—"

"Chris, please!" Beryl almost screamed. "Please let's change the subject. All this talk isn't doing any good anyway. You've already made up your mind."

Danton sat back down again. "That's right. And I'm here tonight to see what you and Louis are going to do. Louis, are you going with Danton Fabrics or staying in this falling-down last outpost of the ante-bellum South? My God, this whole town and everybody in it is an anachronism."

"I don't know, Chris," Louis said. "I'd like a little more time to think about it—to talk it over with Nat. I don't think it makes much difference to her—leaving here, I mean. She'd as soon live in Macontown as here. But it's different with me. My roots are here. I've lived here all my life, and my family before me. It isn't as easy to pull up . . . Well, what I'm saying is I want to think about it a little longer. You don't have to know for a day or two, do you?"

"What about you, Beryl?" Danton said. "I'm sorry you found out about this the way you did— I wanted to tell you myself—but I was afraid I already knew your answer."

Beryl was looking somewhere out over the tops of the bushes, her eyes glazed, with the same faraway expression in them that she got sometimes when she talked to Patrick about Celinda.

"I was just thinking," she said softly. "There won't be a house on Briarman's Cliff now."

"There are hills, cliffs, and even a river near Macontown," Danton said. "You can have any kind of house, anywhere you want it. But I guess I'm expecting too much of you. If you couldn't make up your mind about leaving that crazy family of yours to live right here in Laurelton, you certainly couldn't do it to move two hundred miles away."

"Please, Chris, if only you'd talk to Uncle Darius one more time. Say something to make him understand that it's not only us but everybody in the county who'll suffer. You're so persuasive, I know you can talk him into selling the land if you just try."

"Apparently I'm not persuasive at all. I certainly haven't been able to persuade you—or Louis, for that matter. As for Mr. Quincannon, I haven't one word left to say to that son of a bitch. And if I had known Louis was going there this afternoon I think I'd have tried to stop him. But anyway, we all have his answer, and I consider it final. You and your sister can't sell your shares of the property because he won't let go of his. So that, my friends, is that." He stood up again.

"I've had it up to here with this whole business. I'm leaving now, but I want to tell you something, all of you. I want an answer by tomorrow night. Louis, you can let me know if you'll be manager at the new plant in Macontown, and Beryl," he paused and his voice was a little softer when he continued, "Beryl, I still want to marry you and I want you to come to Macontown with me. But I'm not going to wait any longer for you to decide which magnolia bush you want to pick the blossoms from. Tomorrow night, and I mean it. Goodnight, Natalie."

He went inside the house, followed by Natalie, and out the front door. Louis and Beryl sat looking at each other without saying a word, and then Louis got up and walked out into the back yard, leaving Beryl.

Patrick wanted to go to her, but he didn't know what he would say if he did. There was nothing anybody could say. Rusty nudged him and motioned for him to go back through the japonicas. They snaked their way out, to the side of the house.

"Mama's going to call me in a minute, so I thought we'd better get out of there," Rusty said. "Patrick, what do they mean about leaving here? Why has anybody got to leave? Why is Chris going to move the plant? Why can't we just stay here the way we are, the way we've been planning all the time?"

Patrick could not say a word. He could not possibly tell his friend that Uncle Darius was the reason for everybody's bad luck. Suddenly he wanted to cry. He felt the tears coming and turned his head so Rusty couldn't see. Fortunately, at that moment Danton's car pulled out of the driveway, and Natalie yelled, "Rus-tee, time to come in now and get your bath. Rusty, where are you?"

"I've got to go, but you'll come over tomorrow, won't you?" Rusty said.

Patrick nodded, still not looking at his friend.

His steps going home were even slower than his steps coming over. He was still trying to hold back the tears, and now there was a new worry. He felt sick to his stomach, really sick. He walked a little faster when he neared the Quincannon block, trying to get home before he threw up. It couldn't have been the rice pudding, he thought. He never had liked the stuff, but he'd hardly touched it tonight.

He was almost at the gate when he knew he was not going to make it to the house. Holding the iron spikes of the fence, he put his head into the ivy and vomited, again and again, and when nothing else would come up he still kept retching.

Finally it stopped, and he leaned weakly against the fence. Then he took a spike in each hand and shook with all his might, crying, "Dammit, dammit, dammit, DAMMIT!" Even all his weight against the iron failed to cause the slightest tremor of fence or gate. They were firm, unmoving.

# 18

When Beryl came in that night, Patrick was in her bed asleep. When he was awakened, he wasn't quite sure where he was, or why. Then, as it all came back to him, he murmured sleepily with no hope of success, "Beryl, you wouldn't want to finish the rest of the story now, would you?"

Beryl laughed mirthlessly. "You mean about Celinda? It's late, Patrick. Maybe later than any of us think."

"I don't care what time it is."

"Youth has time to squander," she said, and he knew she wasn't really talking to him at all. But then she said, "Why not? All right, Patrick, at this point it doesn't make much difference to me what you know or don't know. Where did we stop before?"

He couldn't quite believe it. This wasn't at all the attitude he had expected Beryl to take. But then, he had never seen Beryl like this before.

"Celinda went away with Jaybird—I mean Jason." In spite of the fact that he was beginning to think of his father as Jaybird for the first time, he didn't want to. And he wasn't sure why.

"After Celinda left," Beryl said, "the months dragged by, day after endless day, and Uncle Darius' wishes were respected. Sometimes when Mavis and I were alone in the kitchen, we talked about Cee, wondered where she was and if she was happy. But with Uncle Darius and Athena, the name of Celinda was not spoken. And there were no letters from her, no word, nothing.

"And then when she came back the time went by so fast that after it was all over it was like a terrible dream you only partially remember after waking— the kind of strange dream in which everything is distorted.

"She didn't come back in the red car, she came back on the bus and then got a taxi to the house. And do you know? I don't think anybody ever even thought to ask her what happened to the car." Beryl said this as though the thought had just occurred to her for the first time. "I wasn't quite sure what kind of reception she received. I came home from the shop, a bit alarmed because Uncle Darius had not met me and I thought something might have happened to him. Mavis met me at the front door.

"'She's back, Miss Beryl. Praise God, she's back!'

"I didn't have to ask who. 'When, Mavis? And where is she?'

"'Sometime during the afternoon, they said. She was already here when I came to fix supper. They're all in the library now, shut up in there.'

"I rushed to the library and opened the door. The three of them were having such a serious conversation that they didn't hear me come in. Uncle Darius was seated at the desk in almost the exact position he had been in the night Celinda left. Athena sat in the harpback chair beside him, and there in the big overstuffed chair where Uncle Darius has his afternoon naps was Celinda, hunched down low in the chair and looking very pale and tiny and somehow lost, as though by mistake she had stumbled onto the wrong planet and wasn't sure how to rectify the error.

"'How do we know you're back for good?' Uncle Darius was saying. 'How do we know you're not going right back to that—that scoundrel?'

" 'He doesn't want me back,' Cee said, in a small voice. 'I think maybe he wants to get married, although he didn't say so. There's a woman—extremely rich, I hear—he's been seeing.'

" 'Get married!' Uncle Darius shouted. 'In the name of God, isn't he married to you?'

" 'Yes, of course.'

" 'Then how can he marry somebody else?' Athena asked. 'I thought the Catholic Church didn't allow divorce.'

" 'Jay's not a very good Catholic,' Cee said. 'I guess . . .' her voice became even smaller, 'he isn't a very good anything.' "

Beryl stopped suddenly and looked at Patrick, and he could tell she was trying to decide whether to go on, because no matter what she thought of Jaybird Tolson, Patrick was his son. He had to convince her it was all right.

"Jaybird was a yellow-livered bastard, wasn't he?" he said calmly, expecting her first reaction to be shock at his using a bad word and her second to be one of censuring him. What she said was, "Yes, something like that."

There was a moment of silence, then she said, "I couldn't stand it any longer. I had to make my presence known. I ran to Cee and cried, 'Welcome, welcome home.'

"She jumped and so did the other two, then she got up and threw her arms around me. 'You can't imagine how much I've missed you,' she said.

"When she stood up, I noticed for the first time that she was going to have a baby."

Patrick looked down at the rug.

"During the next two months Cee and I had many long talks," Beryl said, not noticing Patrick at all. "And no matter what subject the conversation began on, it eventually drifted back to Jason Tolson.

"'I don't know why I ever thought I loved him,' she said one night when she was in here sitting on my bed. 'And I knew all along that he never loved me.'

"'Then why, Cee, why for the Lord's sweet sake did you go away with him?'

"'I had to go away, Berry. If you'll think about it for a while, you'll understand. I was suffocating here. You all were smothering me to death. Uncle Darius especially, but even you and Athena.'

"'What do you mean?' I asked her. 'I wasn't aware of any suffocation.'

"'That's just it, none of you were, and it was something I didn't know how to explain then, not even to myself. I'm not sure I can now. But all my life—as long as I can remember—all of you have treated me as though I were the only person in the world who meant anything to you. None of you had lives of your own, you lived your lives through me. It was—well, it was too much of a responsibility for me. I kept thinking, someday I'll let them down because I can never be all they expect of me. And I kept thinking, if I weren't here they'd have lives of their own, something else to focus on. And sometimes it was maddening because I had no life of *my* own. Everytime I left the house there were four of you—yes, even Mavis —clustered around wanting to know where I was going and when I'd be back and what I was going to do and whom I was going to see. And even when you learned I didn't like this and wouldn't tell much, I still couldn't leave the house, even to run a quick errand downtown, that I didn't feel all of the unasked questions following me.'

"She was quiet for a while, then she said, 'It's not that I was totally ungrateful, Berry, and didn't appreciate all the attention and love—if that's what it was. But it was too much. I had to get away, and I don't think I realized the reason until after I did go away. I had so much time to think then, while we were in Buffalo. That's such a cold town, in so many ways. Jason used to go to New York for weekends, but he never took me.'

"'All right, Cee,' I said, 'granted we wouldn't let you have a life of your own here and you had to get away. Why of all the people in the world did you go away with Jason Tolson? He was one of the most indifferent souls I've ever met, and I only had to see him once to know this.'

"'There's your answer right there,' Cee said. 'He *was* indifferent. In fact, he made such a good job of letting me alone that it was a challenge to me. I'd never been treated like that before and at first it was refreshing and then, as I said, it became a challenge. Jason never wanted to marry me, so that made me want to marry him desperately. I guess that's why I can't—why I shouldn't—feel bitter about the way it's all turned out.'

"'Doesn't he have any feeling about the child you're going to have?'

"Celinda shook her head. 'The baby wasn't his

idea either.' She was quiet for a long time as she seemed to be remembering. Then she looked up suddenly and said, 'We had a terrible fight the night I left. We said things—well, it doesn't matter now what was said, but the worst of it was that it was all the truth, every terrible thing he said and every terrible thing I said. And then I had one of what Mavis used to call my spells. I broke everything in that apartment that was breakable. I don't think there was anything left intact. If he forgets everything else about me, he'll remember that night. Not a very nice way to be remembered, is it?'

" 'Your disillusionment with him must have been unbearable,' I said.

" 'I wasn't disillusioned,' she said, 'because I never had any illusions in the first place. I was disillusioned with myself. I didn't want to come back here, Berry, but there was nowhere else to go—seven months pregnant and no money, not a cent in the world.'

"I tried very hard during the short time Cee was with us to read Uncle Darius' mind, or at least get some slightest indication of what he was thinking, but it was impossible. Before, his thoughts had been fairly transparent, especially when Cee was around, but now they were so veiled with caution that I sometimes wondered if he himself knew what he was thinking. He did not look at Celinda in the same way he had before—sometimes he would lower his eyes when she came into the room where he was. I don't know whether this was because he was afraid she would leave again or whether he was merely embarrassed by her pregnancy.

"And then it was all over so quickly that I was hardly aware of what was happening, and even later when there was time—nothing but time—to try to sort the events, the few words spoken, the many, many thoughts, there was still nothing that happened in those last two days that had any reality for me.

"Dr. Armbruster was called to the house at eleven o'clock on a Friday night and you, Patrick, were born at ten o'clock the next morning. Celinda had refused to go to the hospital, saying she wanted her baby to be born in the Quincannon house. I don't know why, this just seemed to be an idea she came up with at the last minute—as though this house represented the only security she had ever known and she was suddenly afraid to leave it.

"Uncle Darius, Athena, and I waited in the living room. We waited and waited. Finally, after what seemed hours—*was* hours—the nurse came downstairs and said, 'Dr. Armbruster wants me to call an ambulance to take Mrs. Tolson to the hospital. She still refuses to go, but the doctor said if we get your permission we can take her anyway. She doesn't know what's best for her right now.'

"'Is she in danger?' Uncle Darius asked.

"'Dr. Armbruster thinks she should be in the hospital where everything is at hand if—'

"'We will do what Celinda wants,' Uncle Darius

said. 'If she wants to stay here, we'll see that she is not moved.'

"Uncle Darius turned his back on the nurse, and she went back upstairs. She didn't come down again until after you were born, Patrick. She said Cee needed a transfusion, and we should get her to the hospital immediately. And Uncle Darius said to give her the transfusion right here, because he was not going to let them take Celinda out of the house.

"They did what they could. Sometime during the afternoon, Dr. Armbruster came downstairs. He said that Cee was better, that she had a chance.

"'May I see her?' I asked.

"'She's asleep now, but you can see the baby.'

"In our anxiety over Cee, not one of us had thought to ask about you, Patrick, and by then you were about five hours old.

"I asked the doctor where you were.

"'We put the bassinet in your room this morning,' he said.

"I went upstairs and looked at the wicker basket at the foot of my bed. You had a tiny, wrinkled, red face, Patrick, and you were sleeping, peacefully unaware of the chaos in the house. Your hair was long and silky and dark, and your eyes were tightly closed little slits. There was nothing about you that reminded me of Celinda. I looked at you for a long time, feeling so sorry for you.

"When I left the room, I saw Dr. Armbruster in the hall. He said, 'She's awake now and she's asking for you. She doesn't want to see Athena or Darius, just you. And don't stay in there long, Beryl. I don't want her exerting herself. I'm going now, but I'll look in tonight about bedtime.'

"I stood beside her bed for a while before she opened her eyes and smiled at me. 'Have you seen him?' she asked.

" 'The baby? Yes, I just saw him.'

" 'His name is Patrick,' Cee said. 'Patrick Quincannon Tolson. Will you do something for me, Berry?'

" 'Of course, Cee. What?'

" 'Look after Patrick for me. Don't let him be avalanched the way I was by all of you. Don't let Uncle Darius or Athena or even yourself—well, don't let his life be the way mine was. Please.'

" 'You can see to that yourself, Cee. You'll be up soon and—'

" 'And promise me something else, Berry. Promise me you'll have a life of your own now, too. Don't try to live in and through someone else the way . . .' She broke off.

" 'Cee, stop this. You're going to be all right, and you know it. Now stop trying to scare me to death.'

"She smiled and nodded and said, 'Promise anyway.'

" 'All right, I promise.'

" 'Thank you. Now will you please call Father Conroy and ask him to come.'

" 'No, Cee. You're all right. Really you are. Dr. Armbruster said you'd be all right now.'

" 'Just call him for me, Berry. I want to see him.'

"I went downstairs and told Athena and Uncle Darius that Cee had asked for the priest.

"'Wait until tomorrow,' Athena said. 'No point in bothering him now. Celinda needs rest more than she needs to talk about her religion.'

"'I don't want him to come here,' Uncle Darius said. 'Jason Tolson has done enough to her without inflicting his church on her, too.'

"In the middle of the night Celinda began to hemorrhage again, and by the time Dr. Armbruster got there she was unconscious. Uncle Darius, Athena, and I stood outside her door, looking miserably from one to the other, not knowing who needed comfort most or what comfort there was to give.

"I couldn't stand to look at Uncle Darius' face. It was like nothing human. I went downstairs, hardly aware of what I was doing, and stopped in the hall beside the telephone. I looked up the number of St. Anne's rectory and called. It seemed ages before a sleepy voice answered and I said, 'Father Conroy? This is Beryl Quincannon. I think my sister is dying. Can you come? She asked for you.'

"Just before dawn, Cee regained consciousness and Dr. Armbruster left the room so Father Conroy could hear her confession and give her the last rites of the church. Then he opened the door and talked for a minute with Dr. Armbruster, then to us.

"'She wants her baby baptized now, and Dr. Armbruster says you may come inside.'

"We went in and stood at the foot of the bed,

watching Cee and then you, Patrick, as the priest made the sign of the cross on your forehead and said, 'Patrick Quincannon Tolson, I baptize you in the name of the Father and of the Son and of the Holy Spirit.' Then there were prayers, and we all looked at the calm face of the priest and listened to his deep voice.

"It happened sometime during the prayers. When we looked at Celinda again, we knew she had left us for the last time."

Beryl was quiet for so long that Patrick thought she was not going to speak again. In a way, he hoped she wouldn't. He didn't think he could stand to hear any more about Celinda.

"It was over," she said finally. "Everything. There was no bitterness toward one another among the three of us left, because each was too busy with individual grief to place blame or make accusations or even give thought to the others. We tried to act as we had right after Cee's elopement, but it wasn't the same now. Mavis took care of you during the day, and I was there at night. I think I was the first to begin to emerge from shock. Uncle Darius spent more and more time with his scrapbooks and paste-ups, and one month after Cee's death he decided it was time he retired from the bank, so that left him the days as well as the nights to indulge his hobby.

"It was during one of those long, quiet evenings that I finally realized what Cee had meant when she told me to start living a life of my own. I didn't want to be like Athena, who never seemed to care much about anything, and I didn't want to be like Uncle Darius, who had cared too much for a few things. Somewhere I had to find the way for myself.

"Uncle Darius' reaction to Cee's death was completely different from his reaction to her elopement. His eyes remained dry and cold and appraising, as though he was sizing up the whole world and finding it wanting, and finding nothing left in it that was worth his emotion.

"I also expected him to hate you, Patrick, with a hatred that goes beyond human boundaries. I thought he would think of you as Jaybird's son and perhaps even a cause of Cee's death. Or else, I thought, he would love you the same way he had loved Celinda, because you were her son. Actually, he did neither. He seemed to tolerate you in much the same way he had always tolerated Athena and me. Obviously he considered it his bounden duty to bring you up to be a law-abiding, Christian gentleman who would do nothing to disgrace the Quincannons, so this he's been doing. And nothing more.

"His interest in Athena and me didn't become more pronounced after Cee's death, either. One night shortly after she died, he stood in the middle of the living room with his arms upraised, gesturing to emphasize his points. Now that we had seen what could happen when a girl let herself get carried away by some unprincipled man, he was sure he would not have to tell us to stay at home where we belonged. He said we should preserve the family circle, because that was the only thing worth preserving. He ended his sermon by forbidding us ever to go out with a man. 'If either of you ever feels inclined to leave this house, remember your dead sister. She went away, and she learned what a wrong thing she had done. Why do you think she refused to go to a hospital? Because she never wanted to spend another night away from this house, that's why.'"

Something was bothering Patrick, had been bothering him for several minutes. "Beryl," he said, "if I was baptized and made a Catholic almost as soon as I was born, why did I always go to the Methodist church? Why didn't anybody ever tell me I was a Catholic?"

"Uncle Darius' first act after Cee died was to order Father Conroy out of the house. 'While you were standing there saying all that mumbo jumbo over the baby, Celinda died,' he said. 'I suppose you had already filled her full of Latin bromides, so it was all right to ignore her while you chalked up another soul for your church. Well, let me tell you something. You may have gotten her, but you won't get this baby. Not while there's breath in my body. That's one thing I can do for Celinda. See that her baby is kept out of the church his good-for-nothing father belongs to.'

"'It was also the church of his mother,' Father Conroy said, 'and she wanted her son to grow up in her church, or she wouldn't have asked me to baptize him before she died.'

"And while the priest was trying to show Uncle Darius the logic of his argument, Uncle Darius showed him the door.

"There was nothing Uncle Darius could do about Cee's funeral, except, of course, refuse to go. Even Athena agreed with me that Cee should have a requiem Mass and be buried in the Catholic cemetery. 'She wanted Father Conroy at the end,' Athena said, 'and she would want the rest of it this way. For once, we'll have to go against Uncle Darius' wishes.'

"So while Mavis stayed at the house with you, and Athena and I went to the Catholic Church, Uncle Darius walked into the woods behind the house and did not return for six hours. When he came in he said, 'It's done, I suppose. You and Athena saw it through. Well, we won't mention it again. I am going to have a monument for Celinda put up in the grove back there. It is quiet, and it is a pretty spot, and it is Quincannon property, not Catholic property. I think Celinda would have wanted it for her final resting place, and so it shall be. This is where she found her true rest.'

"The next day he selected the monument, and a week later, when the inscription had been chiseled on, it was placed in the woods. At first Uncle Darius walked into the woods daily, and then the walks were less frequent, and soon the time came when he hardly ever went to the woods, but by that time the idea seemed to be firmly entrenched in his mind that his beloved Celinda really lay resting under the oak tree where he had played as a child, and we would sooner have disturbed her rest than disturb this idea which, finally, brought the first semblance of peace to his mind.

"Celinda, Beloved Daughter of Donald and Sarah Quincannon. *Requiescat in Pace.*"

Beryl stopped talking abruptly, jumped as though she had been startled out of a deep sleep, then said, "Now you know, Patrick. Now you know everything."

"Yes."

"I hadn't planned to tell you all of it. Not for years anyway. Do you know why I did?"

"No, not really. Why did you, Beryl?"

"Because it doesn't make any difference now." She put her hands to her face and burst into tears, something Patrick had never seen her do in his entire life. "Nothing in this whole damn world makes any difference any more!"

Her shoulders were shaking, and he could see the tears trickling between her fingers. He wanted to do something, to say something, but what can you say to a grownup who cries like a child?

"Beryl . . ."

She didn't even know he was in the world now.

"Beryl . . ."

He stood up and edged toward the door. "I guess I'll go to bed now, Beryl."

He waited and waited, and he knew he couldn't stand the sight of Beryl crying any longer. "Goodnight, Beryl. Thank you for telling me."

He fled to the privacy of his own room where no one would know whether he cried or not. He sat on the window seat, looking toward the dark, dark woods, and repeated Beryl's words. "Nothing in this whole damn world makes any difference any more."

# 19

"Patrick, what are you, crazy or something? I don't see why you can't go." There was a pause. "Unless you're being punished. Have you done something bad again?"

"I can't go this time, Rusty, so there's no need to keep on about it. I just can't go. Maybe next time."

"School starts next month, so there may not *be* a next time," Rusty said. "What kind of reason do you want me to give Daddy? You want me to say, 'Patrick just don't want to go fishing any more?'"

Patrick sighed. Sometimes Rusty really showed how young he was. "If you must know, I can't go anywhere until I figure something out."

"What you figgering? On digging up some more graves?"

"That won't be necessary," Patrick said stiffly. "Rusty, don't be so *child*ish."

Rusty, hurt, looked away. "I didn't mean nothing by it, Patrick. I guess I'm just as sorry as you are that you didn't find your mother. You figgered out yet whether it's Miss Athena or Miss Beryl? Is that why you won't go with us fishing this weekend, cause you've got to figger that out?"

Patrick sighed again. Someday he would tell Rusty what was what (if Rusty was still around), because after all, Rusty had tried to help when he needed help, but right now he didn't want to be bothered. "What I'm trying to figure right now is how to get rid of Beryl."

"God's pink necktie, Patrick! You aren't figgering on bumping off Miss Beryl, are you? If you've got to bump off one of them, let it be—"

"Oh, Rusty." Patrick's exasperation knew no bounds. "I'm trying to figure how to make her marry her boy friend, dum-dum."

"Huh, that'll never happen." Rusty nodded wisely and began swinging the creaking swing on the Quincannon porch. "That's all over now. I heard Mama say this morning that Beryl would never decide to go away with Chris. Why do you want her to marry him, Patrick? Mama said Uncle Darius would never let her or Miss Athena get married."

It was a while before Patrick answered. "You'd better go on home now, Rusty. I can't do much figuring with you here asking questions. You tell your daddy I can go on the next fishing trip, maybe in about a week after I get things straightened out here." It made him feel important, like the man of the house, to realize that he was the one who was going to have to straighten things out.

Good-naturedly, Rusty got out of the swing. "Okay, Patrick, I'll see you tomorrow—maybe."

Patrick waited until Rusty was out of sight and then he left the porch and went to the sidewalk. He hadn't any plans when he told Rusty to leave, but now he knew exactly where he was going. Since

Beryl finished her story last night, he had given a great deal of thought to Celinda. Now, he wanted to go to the florist's shop and spend the allowance he'd been saving for a new fishing rod on some flowers for Celinda's grave. He had planned on red roses, but when he got to the shop and saw the yellow roses, they looked so much like Celinda that he knew he would not be satisfied with anything else.

When he reached the cemetery, he thought again of the tombstone in the woods behind the Quincannon house. He thought and thought, but he still didn't quite know what to make of it. Except what he had been thinking for a long time: that the whole family was screwy as hell. But no, he couldn't include them all in that. Uncle Darius seemed a little teched at times, especially since Beryl had told Patrick everything, and Athena—well, maybe she was just a little bit off now and then, but Beryl certainly was all right enough. There was nothing wrong with her.

And when he *really* thought about it, was it strange that Uncle Darius should have loved Celinda the most? She was Patrick's mother, the most beautiful person who had ever lived, and the nicest and everything, so why *shouldn't* Uncle Darius have loved her the most and been all broken up when she died? He, Patrick, had not even known her, and he had always loved her the most.

He sat down in the grass beside the grave. It was funny, the way things turned out. Only a little while ago he thought he had lost Celinda forever, but now he had her again. God had given her back to him. The prayer he had thought too hopeless to pray had been answered anyway. It was as much a miracle as closing the jaws of a lion or having water turned into wine. Celinda was his mother again, and he did not have to change the image of her in his mind.

It was up to him now to carry out Celinda's wishes, since no one else seemed to know how to go about it. He didn't either, but maybe if he figured on it long enough, he could come up with something. When Celinda told Beryl to lead a life of her own, she had meant for Beryl to get away from that old house. He knew that as surely as he knew anything. And he also knew that he, Patrick, was the reason Beryl had stayed. Beryl was pretty old now, and if she didn't get away quick she might not ever have another chance. And he would always be the main reason for her staying. He couldn't have this on his mind for the rest of his whole, entire life. He had to figure something right now.

"Hello, Patrick. I thought I saw you pass the rectory."

"Hello, Father."

The priest squatted on the grass beside him. "Did you bring the roses? They're very pretty."

"I brought them because they look like Celinda."

"You're right. They do." He looked at Patrick as though Patrick were a different person. "Did you talk to your aunt?"

Patrick nodded. "Beryl told me all about Celinda and everything." He was quiet for a minute, then he said, "I think I know what that choice was you were talking about, it was whether I should go to the Methodist church or yours, wasn't it?"

"What do you think, Patrick? Is there a choice?"

"I don't know. I guess not. I've always been a Catholic, haven't I? Ever since I was three days old."

"Yes."

"I've been thinking I might go to your church this Sunday. I never went to a real service there before."

"Does your Uncle Darius know of your plans?"

"Not yet, but I guess he will pretty soon."

"Then I suppose I can expect a call from him." The priest sighed. "But regardless of his attitude, you should be allowed to learn about your mother's faith."

Patrick stood up. "Don't worry about Uncle Darius," he said with more assurance than he felt. "I can manage him all right. I better go now, it's about time for Athena to start looking for me for supper."

He went a few steps down the path between the graves, then turned back to the priest who was standing now, looking down at the roses. "Father, would you tell me something honestly and truly if I asked you?"

"As honestly and truly as I can, Patrick."

"Did my mother turn Catholic before or after she met Jay—my father?"

Father Conroy looked surprised at the question. He scratched a red spot on the end of his big nose as he thought. "I think it was before, Patrick. I remember it was during the summer that I gave her instruction, and I don't think Jason Tolson came to town until late summer or early fall. Yes, I'm sure it was before."

"Okay," Patrick said. "I just wanted to know."

He sat on the high stool in the kitchen watching Mavis as she put the biscuits in the oven and dished up the vegetables for supper.

"Mavis, that really was a picture of Celinda you showed me, wasn't it?"

"Patrick, what kind of devilment you starting now? I heard enough about that picture."

"But it *was* Celinda, wasn't it?"

"I told you it was at the time, Mr. Know-it-all."

"Then why'd you say later that it was Beryl?"

"I didn't say it, *you* said it." Mavis looked indignant.

"You said it, too," Patrick said. "That night while we were eating supper I asked you if it was Beryl and you said yes. Why'd you do that?"

"'Cause I didn't want Mr. Darius to know I still had a picture of Miss Cee. He told us all to throw away our pictures."

"Mavis, I wonder—would you let me have that picture? I'll buy it from you. I'll give you all of my allowance for a whole, entire month."

Mavis stopped in the midst of spooning up the turnip greens. "You forget about that picture before you get in some more trouble, Patrick. I don't aim to be the one who helps you in, either."

"Please, Mavis. I'll bet it's the only picture of her in all captivity, and I want a picture of my mother."

He could tell she was relenting. "I don't know, Patrick. Maybe. Maybe if you'll be good, one of these days I'll let you have it."

"Will you bring it tomorrow?"

"I don't know about that. I said if you'll be good."

"I was good today, I'll be good tomorrow."

"Sometimes you tell stories, Patrick. That's not being good."

"Hummph!" he said, sounding like Uncle Darius. "I don't tell half as many stories as some folks I know. Will you bring it tomorrow?"

"Maybe."

He knew that she would.

After supper they sat on the front porch because it was too hot in the living room, with not a breath of air stirring anywhere. Athena and Uncle Darius sat in the green chairs, and Beryl was in the swing. Patrick sat on the top step, his chin resting on his knees.

"Just think," Athena said, "in another month school will start. Where has the summer gone?"

Patrick only wondered why Beryl hadn't gone out to let Danton have an answer to his question.

"It hasn't gone anywhere," Uncle Darius said. "It's right here with us now, and if you can't tell it, there's something wrong with you."

"I was referring to time, not heat," Athena said.

"You should always make yourself clear, Athena," Uncle Darius said, "and even then the chances of being misunderstood are about fifty-fifty."

Beryl sighed.

"What was that for?" Athena asked. "You sounded more than a little weary of us all."

"What it is," Patrick piped up, "is that she's dying of clotted boredom."

There was a short silence, and then Beryl laughed. "You sound like Louis Nichols," she laughed.

"I'm surprised you're not over there tonight," Uncle Darius said. "To what do we owe the honor of your company for so many evenings recently? You and Natalie have a tiff?"

"Of course not. I. . . ." Whatever she was going to say was left unsaid.

I wonder what would happen, Patrick thought, if I said right out that all those times she was supposed to be at the Nichols', she was out with her boy friend, that Yankee fellow who wants to buy our land. I'll bet it would make Uncle Darius so mad that he'd throw Beryl out of the house, and then I wouldn't have to figure any more on how to get her to go.

It would also, he knew, make Beryl mad, and especially at him. This was something he did not want, so he would have to keep figuring to find a way. . . .

"Does seem strange," Athena said, "having you at home every evening for a change."

"Oh, for heaven's sake, let it rest! It's just too hot." Beryl's voice was almost a whisper. "Too hot to go anywhere."

Patrick raised his head and looked at her. Her

eyes were glistening with what looked like tears, but in the darkness he couldn't be sure.

"One of these days, you'll learn," Uncle Darius said. "You'll learn that home and family are all that really count and that these strangers you see—"

"They're not strangers," Beryl said. "They're my friends."

"Home and family," Uncle Darius said again. "You'll learn."

Patrick looked up again, and this time he *was* sure Beryl was crying. If he was going to do anything, anything at all to help her, he ought to get started right now.

He got up and went in the house.

"Where are you going, Patrick?" Athena called.

"To get a drink of water," he said. That must have been the way they kept after Celinda all the time. Where are you going now? What are you going to do?

"Don't you think you could be a little bit polite if you put your mind to it?" Athena asked.

"Would anyone else like some water?" he said.

"No, thank you," Athena said immediately, and the others didn't bother to answer.

Patrick stopped in the front hall by the telephone. He had not gone nearly far enough in his figuring, but he knew he was either going to have to do something without figuring or else start figuring faster, because there was something about Beryl that scared him. Ever since last night, when she had finished the Celinda story.

Both she and Louis Nichols were supposed to give Christopher Danton their answers tonight. That meant that Danton probably was at the Nichols' house waiting for Beryl. He dialed the number, disguised his voice—successfully, he hoped—and asked to speak to Mr. Danton. When Danton came to the phone, he said, "This is Patrick Tolson." Pause. "You know, I'm Beryl Quincannon's . . . Yes, that's right. Could you come here tomorrow night? Yes, here to the house, about eight o'clock. No, Uncle Darius didn't ask me to call you. I'm calling for Beryl." Long pause. "Yes, I'm serious, you come on in the house. We'll see you at eight o'clock."

He went back out to the porch and sat down and resumed his figuring.

# 20

The day dragged like a snail slowed by a virus. Early in the morning Patrick plopped himself down on the back steps again in his thinking position, elbows propped on knees, hands cupping his chin. By eight o'clock tonight he had to come up with a solution not only for Beryl but also for the whole, entire family, because he knew now that there was much more involved than just getting Beryl to admit that Christopher Danton was her boy friend. He wondered briefly what Louis Nichols' answer to Danton had been last night. Since Beryl hadn't gone out last night, her answer was no, and that was the main thing Patrick had to change. He couldn't have Beryl staying with this screwy family because of him. Celinda wouldn't have wanted it.

He sat on the steps all morning and began to experience the feeling of panic for the first time in his life. Every passing minute made him feel more helpless and inadequate for the job that had to be done. If only he knew how to begin. . . .

"Patrick, you sick or something?" Mavis had come out to the back porch and was standing behind him, hands on her hips.

"Let me alone, Mavis. I'm thinking."

"You must have a powerful lot to think about."

He turned around suddenly. "Did you bring the picture?"

"What picture?"

"You know good and well what picture. The picture of Celinda you promised me."

"I don't recall making any promises, mister. I learned a long time ago not to promise—"

"Did you bring it? Answer me yes or no."

"I brought it, but I haven't decided. . . ."

He stood up and held out his hand, "Come on, Mavis. You brought it for me, so you might as well give it to me. Please."

Mavis reached into the pocket of her apron. With a sigh, she looked at the small snapshot once before she gave it to him. "All right, but you've got to promise you won't get me into any trouble. I was supposed to throw it away years ago."

He sat down on the steps again, clutching the picture.

"I can't make any promises either, but I'm not looking for any trouble. It may come, but I'm not looking for it on purpose."

"Miss Athena sure got your number, Patrick. She said when you sit quietly like that all the little devils inside you are holding a summit conference. What sort of mischief you planning now?"

He didn't answer, and after a while she went back into the kitchen, muttering something about idleness being the devil's workshop.

Later in the morning he heard Uncle Darius calling him, but he did not answer. He had forgotten all about the paste-ups after breakfast, and he knew that was why Uncle Darius was looking for him. He held his breath, waiting to see if Mavis would tell where he was, but she apparently wasn't going to, because she started singing loudly, "When I wake, wake, wake up in glo-ry. . . ."

He looked at the picture of the little girl with the long hair. When he had first seen the picture, he had thought there was something sad about it. Something about the way the white dress stood out stiffly over the straight, thin legs. But now that he studied the picture, the little girl did not look sad. She was smiling, and he knew intuitively that she was smiling for no other reason than because she was Celinda. Just being Celinda was enough to make her happy.

He put the picture in his pocket and took up his figuring again.

During the afternoon he walked over to the cemetery behind St. Anne's. He was hoping Father Conroy would see him and come out and talk, but the priest did not appear, and Patrick wasn't sure what he wanted to talk about anyway, so he went back home, nursing his growing panic with more panic. By late afternoon he wanted only to go to bed and forget everything, including the fact that he had appointed himself master of ceremonies for the evening's program. But Christopher Danton would be there at eight o'clock and he would announce that he was there at Patrick's invitation.

There was no getting out of it; he had to see it through. He went upstairs, washed his face and hands, and changed into a clean shirt, and when Athena called him to supper he went slowly down the stairs.

"You certainly have made yourself scarce today," Uncle Darius said as Patrick held Beryl's chair for her. "The paste-ups are still to be done. I have them ready, so you can put them in the book after supper."

By the time supper is over, Patrick thought, nobody's going to be thinking about any old paste-ups.

He nodded, then bowed his head while Uncle Darius asked the blessing.

"You will have chicken, won't you, Patrick?" Athena asked.

"Yes, thank you." Not even the drumstick looked good to him tonight. He closed his eyes and prayed for inspiration to know how to begin what must be begun, but either the direct dialing system wasn't working or he was getting a wrong number, because no inspiration came. God was too busy watching sparrows. . . .

He opened his eyes, focused somewhere on the wall above Beryl's head, and said, "I went to my mother's grave today."

"Are the mole tracks still there?" Uncle Darius asked.

"I went to my mother's grave in the Catholic cemetery."

Uncle Darius' fork clattered to his plate, Athena gasped, and Beryl turned pale. No one seemed to know how to end the stunned silence that followed, so Patrick said, as casually as he could, "Those aren't mole tracks out back, Uncle Darius. It's where I dug."

"*Dug?* Dug what?" Uncle Darius wasn't even blinking his wide, staring eyes.

"I wanted to see if Celinda was really buried there, so I dug until I found out she wasn't. Then I found out where she was really buried."

Athena gasped again, and Beryl looked as though she wanted to be excused.

Uncle Darius rose from the table like lava from an erupting volcano. "What do you mean?" he shouted. "Celinda's grave is in the woods behind the house."

"Celinda's grave is behind St. Anne's Church," Patrick said quietly. "She was a Catholic and— and I'm a Catholic."

"What has that priest been telling you?" Uncle Darius' voice got louder with every question. "I'll break his neck for this."

"Father Conroy didn't tell me," Patrick said.

"Mavis! Come in here," Uncle Darius called.

"Mavis didn't tell me either," Patrick said,

squirming under Uncle Darius' discomforting gaze.

"Mavis, what have you been telling this boy?" Uncle Darius asked when Mavis appeared at the door.

"Nothing, Mr. Darius, I swear I didn't tell him a thing." Mavis looked as though she wanted lightning to strike her. She stepped back toward the swinging door. "If he knows anything he found out from somebody else. He asked me for the picture, and honest, Mr. Darius, I didn't mean to do anything wrong, but I thought it wouldn't do any harm for him to have a picture of his mother."

"What picture?" By now Uncle Darius' face was as purple as a purple Easter egg that had once made Patrick sick. "What picture?"

Patrick took the picture from his pocket. "This one. This picture of Celinda."

Uncle Darius was beside him in one step and took the picture from his hand. "I ordered that all these . . ." he began, and then he stopped. His shoulders sagged and he went slowly to his chair and sat down, panting for breath.

"I'm sorry, Mr. Darius," Mavis said softly. "I just couldn't burn Miss Cee's picture. It was the only one I had."

Athena looked first at Patrick and then at Uncle Darius. "Patrick, how could you?" she said. She picked up Uncle Darius' glass of water and gave it to him. "Drink some of this, Uncle Darius."

He knocked the glass out of her hand, and the water spattered across the gray carpet, leaving dark splotches.

Beryl sat like one hypnotized, neither moving

nor speaking. The silence in the room was terrible. Patrick picked up the drumstick and began to gnaw, and Mavis went hastily back to the kitchen.

"Remember something you said, Uncle Darius?" Patrick asked when he finished the drumstick. "You said you'd never sell this land while the remains of one Quincannon were buried here. Well—there isn't one single Quincannon buried here, so I don't see why you won't sell."

No answer.

"So I told Mr. Danton to come here tonight at eight o'clock. I thought maybe you might want to change your mind."

This time it was Beryl who gasped.

"God damn it! Have you lost your mind, boy?" Uncle Darius shrieked, scaring Patrick purple, because this was the first time in his whole, entire life that he'd heard Uncle Darius cuss.

"No, sir. I don't think so," he said, his voice quivering as though he weren't quite sure. "This place is really too big for us. We'll get lost in it, especially after Beryl goes."

All eyes turned toward Beryl, and Beryl asked weakly, "What are you talking about?" and then looked as though she wanted to withdraw the question.

"Beryl is going to get married soon and go to live . . ." He stopped as an idea occurred to him for the first time. If Uncle Darius sold the property, Beryl and Danton wouldn't have to leave town, because Danton Fabrics would still be here. They could build the house they had planned on Briarman's Cliff. "She's going to live somewhere else."

"Beryl," Athena asked, "what on earth is that child talking about?"

Beryl shook her head, unable to speak.

"You know, Uncle Darius," Patrick said confidentially, "it was your fault that Celinda ran away, and if you aren't careful the same thing will happen to Beryl. But she's not going to have to run away, because Christopher Danton is coming to get her tonight."

"Oh, my God!" Athena said.

"What kind of nonsense is this?" Uncle Darius' voice was barely audible now.

"It isn't nonsense," Patrick said. "They want to get married and I don't think you ought to stop them."

Beryl stood up. "Patrick, will you come with me upstairs, please?"

"No, not right now. Mr. Danton will be here in a few minutes. You'd better go get packed, Beryl."

Beryl sat down again. "Rusty," she said softly. "It was Rusty."

Patrick smiled, neither confirming nor denying.

Uncle Darius stared down at the table, whispering over and over, "Celinda, Celinda."

Beryl began to laugh hysterically. "Something has always struck me as being very funny," she said, "and now I can laugh and laugh about it. I don't think I'll ever stop laughing." She wiped the tears from her eyes. "You remember the night Cee died, Uncle Darius. You were rude to Father Conroy, saying something to him about muttering Latin bromides while Cee died. Then you went out and bought a tombstone to mark a phony grave, and you had the biggest Latin bromide of them all put on that stone. *Requiescat in pace.* How in God's name could Cee rest in peace when you've never let her die? You didn't let her live in peace or die in peace."

"Beryl, don't . . ." Uncle Darius appeared to be having trouble talking and breathing at the same time.

"You said it was what Celinda would have wanted, to have a final resting place back there. You were wrong, of course, but Cee did have what she wanted, in spite of you, both in life and in death."

"Beryl, *please!*" Athena said, but Beryl would not be stopped.

"She realized what you—what we all—were doing to her, and she got out. Maybe Jason Tolson was a bastard and the wrong person for Cee, but he was what she wanted at the time. And even more than she wanted him, she wanted to get away from the way we were closing in on her." Beryl took a deep breath. "You're always talking about home and the family circle, but you can't have either without love, and the only love that has been in this house is the love we all had for Cee, and in the end it was that love that killed her, because none of us knew anything about how to love. You never knew, so you couldn't teach us."

When Beryl finished, the others kept staring at her as though she were still talking.

Finally, Patrick said, "So you see, we don't really need this house any more. Celinda isn't here and Beryl will be going and. . . ."

Uncle Darius got up and left the room.

"Patrick, you're a wicked, wicked boy," Athena said. "How could you hurt Uncle Darius like this? And as for you, Beryl—"

"I didn't aim to hurt him," Patrick said, "but he's hurt other people and—"

The sound of the doorbell went through the house like the final gong of judgment.

"That'll be Mr. Danton," Patrick said. "I'll let him in." He turned to Beryl before he left the room. "You don't have to worry about staying here with me, Beryl. Honest you don't. It'll be all right now. You've kept your promise to Celinda, and she would have hated for you to stay here forever and ever."

When he got to the hall, Mavis had already opened the door for Christopher Danton.

"Good evening, Patrick," he said. "I didn't understand that mysterious call last night, but I decided to come anyway."

Uncle Darius came from the library and stood in the back hall, and Athena and Beryl came from the dining room. Uncle Darius looked at Beryl. "Is it true?" he asked. "Is what Patrick says true?"

Beryl looked first at Patrick and then at Chris. She nodded.

"I'm afraid I don't understand . . ." Danton began.

"Are you still interested in buying this property?" Uncle Darius asked.

"Yes," Danton said. "We'll go to one hundred thousand, and that is absolutely our last offer."

"We'll take it," Uncle Darius said and went

upstairs. On the top step he turned. "This place doesn't have any more meaning for us. Nothing does."

"What's he talking about?" Danton asked.

"What he means is, you can have the land and Beryl, too," Patrick said.

Beryl burst into tears and went to Athena. "I don't know what to say," she sobbed.

"I suppose you think I do," Athena said.

Patrick felt as though any minute his stomach might throw up again. "Well, for crying in a bucket, don't just stand there, Beryl, *go*," he screamed.

Beryl looked at Chris again. "Chris—"

"Do you want to go with me, Beryl?"

"Yes, but. . . ."

He threw back his head and laughed. "Then do as Patrick says. Don't just stand there. We can go over to South Carolina and be married tonight."

Beryl stopped long enough to hug Patrick. "Thank you, darling." Then she went upstairs to pack her bag, and Patrick fled into the library and closed the door. He threw himself on the floor behind the big chair and began to cry. His heart was racing the way it did when he ran too fast for a long distance.

In a few minutes Beryl would be gone. He knew she wasn't going for good, that she would come back to Laurelton to live, but it wouldn't be the same. Why, why in tarnation had he done it?

He heard her come downstairs and call him. "Patrick, come say goodbye." But he didn't move. If he went back out in the hall, he'd throw up for sure. He moved in closer behind the chair.

"You can see him when we get back," he heard Danton say. "Thanks, old chap, wherever you are."

"Goodbye, Athena. Will you tell Uncle Darius. . . ." Patrick put his fingers in his ears so he couldn't hear the rest, but even so he heard the front door close when they left.

Weakly, he leaned against the chair. What had he done? Great Jehovah, what had he done?

Finally he stopped crying, but he did not leave his hiding place. He could not face Uncle Darius and Athena yet, so maybe if he stayed behind the chair all night they wouldn't be able to find him. Come morning, Uncle Darius would probably beat him to death with his cane.

He didn't know how long he remained in the cramped position, but after a while he heard movement in the house. He held his breath, expecting them to call him, but there was no sound of voices. Later he heard someone going upstairs, probably Athena, and then someone coming downstairs.

The library door opened and the light was turned on. He peeked around the chair and saw Uncle Darius going toward the desk. Uncle Darius sat down, took a big white handkerchief out of his pocket and blew his nose. Then he opened the scrapbook and began pasting in the pile of clippings beside the book.

Patrick watched in morbid fascination. After everything that had happened, how could Uncle Darius sit there messing with his silly old scrapbook?

When the last clipping was in the book, Uncle Darius took a small square of paper from his pocket and looked at it, then pasted it in the book. He blew his nose again, picked up his fountain pen and wrote something in the book, probably the date, and closed the book. For several minutes he sat staring at the closed book and then, with a huge sigh, he got up, turned out the light, and left the room.

Patrick waited a few minutes until he was sure Uncle Darius had gone back upstairs, then he left his hiding place, turned on the light and went to the desk.

He thumbed through the book until he found the last page that was filled. At the bottom of the page, still damp with paste, was his picture of Celinda. And beneath the picture in Uncle Darius' shaky handwriting was one sentence. *Today I let Celinda go.*

# 21

It was the hottest August anyone could remember, and there were two more weeks of the month to be endured before it would turn into what probably would be the hottest September anyone could remember.

Patrick finished the second session in his instruction from Father Conroy late in the afternoon and left the rectory thinking that today he had had more lemonade than instruction. Even the priest had seemed a little wilted during the afternoon.

Patrick stopped when he reached the sidewalk, spotting a familiar figure standing beside the ivy-covered fence that surrounded the Catholic cemetery on three sides. Uncle Darius was absently fingering a sprig of ivy, looking for all the world as though he wanted to go inside the cemetery but couldn't quite bring himself to set foot on Catholic ground.

"You all through in there?" he asked Patrick.

"Through for today," Patrick said. He fell into step as they started in the direction of home. "Mr. Nichols and Rusty are going on a fishing trip this weekend. Okay if I go?"

"Patrick, how many times do I have to tell you to stop saying okay? There's no such word. Yes, you may go."

They walked along in silence until they reached the iron gate, then Uncle Darius said, "I suppose they will be taking this down, too, along with the fence. Everything."

"Will they bring a wrecking truck and tear down the house and all?" Patrick asked.

"They can't very well put an office building here if the house is still standing."

"Can I watch the wreckers?"

"If you find that proper entertainment."

Patrick was quiet for a minute, then, "That house we bought on Bennett Street, it's a long way from here."

"Yes, we—Athena and I—don't want to stay in this neighborhood."

"It's too far to walk downtown."

"I know. We'll have to get an automobile. Athena is going to learn to drive."

Patrick laughed. The picture of Athena driving a car was the funniest thing he could imagine.

"Never mind, boy," said Uncle Darius. "Athena will do very well. She does everything very well."

"I know." Patrick was silent again, his mind going back to the demolition crew. He could visualize the house going, the fence and the gate. But what about the tombstone in the back yard? What would the crew do when they got to that?

He looked up at Uncle Darius, about to ask him, but the expression on his great-uncle's face made him change his mind. Uncle Darius, who had always seemed ancient to Patrick, now looked old beyond calculation as he stood by the gate looking toward the house.

Patrick wanted desperately to think of something that might cheer Uncle Darius. "Maybe it won't be so bad," he said finally. "Moving out of that old house, I mean."

"It's the end of the Quincannons," said Uncle Darius flatly.

"It's not the end of me, and I'm a Quincannon."

"Your name is Tolson," Uncle Darius said.

Patrick looked down at the ground for one miserable minute, wondering. Am I a Tolson? Or am I a Quincannon? If Jaybird and Celinda weren't really married. . . .

But Uncle Darius had said he was a Tolson—for the first time, too—and so, of course, they must have been married.

He thought about the new house and the old one. The new house was small and flat down on the ground. There was no front porch for him to crawl under, no cool, earthy odor for him to smell, no big back yard with woods. Suddenly he knew exactly how Uncle Darius felt about the old house, and he wanted more than anything in the world to tell him to stop the sale immediately. By saving the house, could the Quincannons be saved also?

But it was too late, he knew that as surely as he knew anything.

Since that night two weeks ago when Chris Danton had taken Beryl away with him, Patrick had missed Beryl something terrible. When she left, it seemed that she had taken so much of the life out of the house with her. He had spent more time in the kitchen with Mavis, because Mavis could be counted on from day to day. But now there was a nagging little fear inside him. What if Mavis didn't like the new house and found another job, what would he have left?

Uncle Darius stopped looking at the house as though he expected it to vanish before his eyes that very minute, gave a long, drawn-out sigh, and started slowly toward the porch. At the steps he turned to Patrick, who had not moved a muscle, and called, "Don't just stand there, boy. It's almost time for supper, and you know we don't like to be kept waiting." Then he went inside, and the screen door closed silently behind him.

Patrick wondered what Celinda would think if she could know what had happened. She would be glad about Beryl, of course, and glad that he had finally found out the truth, wouldn't she?

Celinda, Celinda, Celinda. The name went through his mind like music. If only he had a picture of her to put in his room in the new house. Would Uncle Darius give back the picture in the scrapbook, or at least promise it to him when he died?

An idea occurred to him suddenly. If Mavis had kept one picture hidden, perhaps she had others. He went inside the house and headed straight for the kitchen.

Mavis was getting out the dishes for supper. "There you are, Patrick," she said. "Go get washed up now. Miss Beryl and Mr. Chris are coming for supper."

"Mavis, do you have any more pictures of my mother stashed away?"

"'Course not, Patrick. I gave you the only one I had."

"Are you telling me the truth now?" he asked. She started to speak again, but he silenced her by raising his arms and pointing his finger at her.

"No liar shall enter therein," he thundered. "You remember that, Mavis. If you never remember anything else in your whole, entire life, you remember that."

"Patrick, Patrick, I declare." She shook her head slowly. "There's just no telling what you're going to come out with after one of your thinking spells. And it's still two more weeks before school opens. Jesus God!"